Gypsy Hunted

Andrea Drew

This book is a work of fiction. Names, characters, places and incidents are either the product of the author's imagination or are used fictionally. Any resemblance to actual persons, living or dead, or to actual events or locales is entirely coincidental.

This book is licensed for your personal enjoyment only. This book may not be re-sold or given away to other people. If you like to share this book with another person, please purchase an additional copy for each person you share it with.

DEDICATION

To my three children, for putting life in perspective
and loving me, especially when I least deserved it.
To Stephen, for giving me the support I needed to
write this.
To my Father Eric, for never giving up on my writing
dreams, even when I did.
To Eve, my writing buddy, for brainstorming with me
and helping me give birth to my first Gypsy child.
And to Pete Godfrey, the wizard of words, for
inserting a (metaphorical) rocket up my butt when I
really needed it

A NOTE FROM THE AUTHOR

Although the book is set in Melbourne, Australia, it was written with a view to release on amazon.com primarily for the US market.

For this reason, I have used US spelling.

I hope my readers from Australia and the UK will enjoy the story enough to forgive me.

CONTENTS

ACKNOWLEDGMENTS

Thank you to my editors, Theresa Arkenberg and
Frankie Sutton.
Also to beta readers Amanda Betley, Carrie Wright,
Eve Vennell, John Andrews and Brenda (on
Goodreads)
You all helped to make the story what it is today.

"No one can tell, when two people walk closely
together, what unconscious communication one mind
may have with another" Robert Barr

1

What would you do if you witnessed a kidnapping and found yourself suddenly unable to tell anyone about it? What would you do if the kidnapper was someone that you loved?

*****

On the night I met Connor Reardon, I had barely an instinct, just a hunch, a mere fluttering in the stomach and a warm delicious rush in my chest. I had no idea of what was to come. Of course, none of us knows what's around the corner, not even me, and if I had known, I might have run for the hills. After all, I'm a telepath, not a damn fortuneteller.

It was pitched to me as a casual get together, but something was off. I saw through Chloe's forced off-the-cuff description of the night out. They were setting me up with a random guy. Despite my doubts, I was nervous and had been planning the night out since yesterday. My yellow post it notes that were stuck across the refrigerator in an even line, reassured me that nothing would be forgotten. Oven and cupboards reminded me to check the toaster, heater, and iron, which I had done twice.

I bounced on my toes as I checked my reflection in the mirror. My lipstick didn't seem to be smudged or bleeding and the eye make-up was staying put. I reconsidered my outfit. I'd gone for the classy look, black slim line jeans, dark tailored waistcoat, and a chiffon shirt underneath, sleeves billowing. Cleavage and legs were covered. No time to change now. My nerves were jangling, but then I'd only gotten five hours sleep the night before. I checked my watch again and realized that if I didn't get moving, I'd be late. What felt like a minute, was actually half an hour, and if I didn't get a wiggle on, then my dramatic entrance would be humiliating rather than grand. So, the time had come to get my butt out the door.

As my feet hit the street, I headed off uncertainly. My heels connected with the footpath and I concentrated on not wrenching an ankle. I took a deep breath of the crisp, chilly air, and glanced up as my breath formed globules of mist in front of my face. I blinked and quickened my steps to make up some lost time.

I rubbed my hands down my designer jeans as I noticed my car at the curb—as yet virgin and undriven. Other than Chloe, I hadn't admitted to anyone that I'd spent a fortune on it as motivation to start driving lessons, finally. The driving itself wasn't the problem, more the idea of some lunatic smashing me to smithereens.

As the wind bit into my skin and made my eyes water, I braced. I bowed my head in a vain attempt to buffer the impact and pulled my purple jacket tighter. Despite the large amount of hair spray I'd put in it, my brown hair was blowing across my face, so I pulled up the hood to keep it in check.

Chloe knew I didn't like going out on cold nights. She told me over and over that I should get out more. Granted, I had a track record of not showing up sometimes, but this was winter. I worked from home and had my little world set up there—laptop, heater, stereo, and TV.

As I reached a crossroads, I turned right. The neon signs shone from a couple of hundred meters away. Although I lived so close to the iconic restaurant strip, I very rarely dined there. A table setting for one represented the epitome of all that was ultimate loneliness, and I didn't want to be reminded that I'd split with Mark ten months earlier. I'd mistakenly thought, no, I'd *known* with a certainty that he was the love of my life. After our break up, I learned from the good old grapevine that he'd replaced me within weeks. Adding to my heartbreak, was the knowledge that I'd been the love of his year, not his life.

Deep in thought, I heard the clop of shoes ahead. A woman with short brown hair, which flopped across her forehead, came toward me, with head down and hands around her waist. She reminded me of Leah. The lamplight reflected off her cheekbones, which were a slightly different angle than Leah, but her hair was similar, as was the expression on her face; grim tolerance.

I thought about Renee. Strange as it was, one of my most favorite people in the world was the child of one of my least favorite, my sister, Leah. Leah and I were born eighteen months apart and we grew up as a tight-knit unit, confiding all of our secrets and fears, until puberty set in for me at fourteen. With my hormones rampaging, I was sneaking out bedroom windows to find naughty neighborhood boys and passing quite a bit of alcohol past my lips.

Leah didn't get boobs and the hormone factor until around seventeen, so late that I'd more than once heard Mum comment that she was thinking of taking her to the doctor. So of course, we clashed from that point on. Leah was forever sniping to our parents about what a hormone-fuelled excuse for a sister I was, sneaking out and doing the nasty, while she stayed home like a good little girl, doing what mummy said, basking in the adoration that came with being her favorite. Not just sour grapes, Mum had made it painfully obvious, by buying new clothes and items for her with little regard for my feelings in the matter. Plus, they looked and behaved in sync, so much so that their arguments amused us all. Her relentless spying and blabbing to our parents about what she thought I got up to, came between us.

In my twenties, I moved away from home and I had missed Leah. I decided I'd try a heart to heart to see if I could make up for lost time. I'd grown up and realized I'd acted rashly, but with maturity came thoughts of atoning for the damage, if it was possible. I missed the years as young girls when we had shared everything. However, my attempts to re-discover our lost childhood closeness were too late. We no longer had anything to say to each other.

I had no problems getting along with my niece, Renee. We were the best of friends, despite the fact that I was in my thirties and she was thirteen.

Through the window, I saw Chloe in the far corner and pushed Sophia's Bistro door before realizing the sign said *pull*. Once inside, I paused to unbutton the top of my blouse. The warmth from an open fire on the far wall mingled with the pungent smell of garlic.

"Gypsy! Over here!" shouted Chloe.

She hurried to me, her black bob swaying as she

zigzagged between chairs to plant a dry kiss on my cheek.

I rubbed at it. "Have I got a mark there?"

She frowned slightly as she came around to check.

"No, it's smudge proof lipstick, so it's fine. You scrubbed up pretty well, by the way." Before she turned and strode ahead, I saw the ghost of a smile. I stared at her back, admiring the lemon mohair jacket.

"Come over and grab a glass of wine. I want you to meet a couple of people."

Sophia's was filled nearly to capacity. I glanced at the bar in the corner, admiring the rough-hewn bricks of various shapes and colors, the glasses hanging patiently, and the lights reflecting in the military precision of their shape. A loud hum of voices came from the back room. In a cheesy gesture, signed pictures of Sophia Loren adorned the walls along with Italian flags and a board of photographs. I ran my fingers across my lips and worked on slowing down my breathing, dropping a hand to my stomach. At the table, Chloe led me to faces that I recognized. Rita and Matt from our book club were sitting at the table, and I sat down across from them, acknowledging them with a tight smile and nod, all that I was capable of. My nervousness was peaking, and I could barely concentrate. At last month's book club, Rita had mentioned she was involved in a sizzling 'fling' with a married guy from work, via text only of course, but we'd clashed over it and I wasn't sure yet if I was speaking to her.

To my right, I saw a gorgeous man around my age. I couldn't resist checking, and sure enough, I spotted a white mark where his wedding ring used to be. I decided then and there that I would sit next to him.

To his right was a younger guy, I guessed in his twenties, who shared some facial features, but looked more wiry and wrung-out.

"Gypsy, you know Matt and Rita. This is Connor—" Chloe threw her hand out to my right. "Matt's neighbor and his nephew, Aaron."

Connor nodded politely, a half smile crossing his face as he offered his hand. It felt warm and slightly rough, and I noticed his neatly trimmed nails. He seemed surprisingly tanned for someone of his age. Usually, the tanned folk are in their twenties, or maybe I only noticed my fellow pale-skinned friends.

"Pleased to meet you, Gypsy. Interesting name, I like it." He gestured across with a brown hand, with a pianist's fingers.

Connor's wrinkles were laugh lines, his eyes friendly and bright. Striking brown hair, tanned, handsome face, collared shirt without a tie, the top button undone and the second making a bid for freedom. I tried not to stare at the tantalizing glimpse of his smooth chest. He had a rushed and unfinished air, a rush of something forgotten and left behind. I noticed he was lean, maybe a bit too lean. That was much more easily fixed than being overweight. I could feed him up with my perfectly microwaved meals, or at a pinch, I could always run to my special, canned spaghetti on toast. Cooking and I understand each other well enough to have a natural, mutual aversion.

"Hi," Aaron said quietly, his eyes, within cavernous dark circles, were darting quickly, barely looking up. His skittish demeanor, like a tightly wound machine ready to spring loose, suggested his uncle had dragged him along.

"Have a seat, Gypsy. Happy I managed a night out with all the madness at work." Connor curled his hand around the wine glass and lifted it for another drink. I was mesmerized by his hands, imagining how they would feel if they came close to me.

"It took a bit of persuading, but I'm glad I got here, too." I stared into the open fireplace, hypnotized by the flames, as fragments of the log turned volcano red, only to fall gently as ashy coal.

"Thanks, Chloe." I took the glass of wine pushed toward me and shakily managed a gulp, hoping the spreading warmth would loosen my ill ease.

"It's mesmerizing, isn't it?" said Connor. I brought my head up sharply, turning to him, wondering how he knew, and then realized he had followed my gaze to the open fireplace.

"Oh…um, yes," I said furtively sneaking a glance at him. I prayed that my occasional clumsiness wouldn't rear its ugly head in the next few seconds. "What do you do, Connor?"

"I'm a police detective."

"A detective? I had you pegged as a professor," I said, loosening up now. Warmth rose from my feet to my legs and torso. My bag was slung across the back of the chair and I gave it a pat. Shoes and bags could be relied upon to offer comfort in my weaker moments. Connor chuckled quietly, and then his shoulders dropped as he leaned across the table toward me. He had moved so close that his eyebrows, wisps of brown, lowered, and he fussed with his earlobe, tugging and rubbing at it, almost wishing it away.

"It's been a big change separating from Jill. I saw you looking at the mark on my finger. A colleague said I reminded him of Robinson Crusoe. I had hoped he meant my rough around the edges look more than anything else, but I think he meant the isolated and being on my own factor. Some days, a desert island sounds appealing, I must admit."

He glanced at me before squeezing his knee. He seemed to be holding his breath. I admired his chin, the smoothness of it. There was nothing better than a freshly shaved man, especially one with a whiff of classy cologne about him. I had no patience for beards, and if we were going to get lip to lip at some point, I'd rather not have scratchy facial hair leaving me with nasty gravel rash.

Aaron seemed awkward and alone, his gaze ping ponging without making eye contact, his mouth opening and closing as he struggled to find words, one fair curl stuck to his forehead with glittering sweat.

"What about you, Aaron?" I asked, wanting to include him in our conversation. "What do you do for a living?"

His dirty fingernails were curled under his rough hands, so that the dead skin was visible. Noticing my attention, he quickly withdrew them to his lap. "Um…a laborer, you know. It's not rocket science, but I guess it's a job."

"That's true, at least you've got one."

His lips pressed together in a slight grimace and he swallowed, magnifying his discomfort. There was something that I picked up about him, his odd conversation, or something that was not quite right.

As a telepath, I notice feelings and instinct more than most. Other people like to call me a psychic medium, but I'm not comfortable with that label.

Apart from the fact that I do it for love, not money, I'm sure that once someone learns I'm a telepath, they conjure up images of dodgy fraudsters on stage at mass events, feeding grieving families what they desperately need. I'd rather not expose myself to more ridicule than necessary. My abilities happened almost by accident—apparently my grandmother was 'fey,' as my mother enjoyed mentioning.

I was sure the pinging, nagging doubt had something to do with Aaron's home life. "What about you, Gypsy? What do you do?" Connor relaxed his posture, the glass poised before his mouth. He had taken on a different look, probably from the wine, or even better, from unfulfilled lust.

"I write business plans. I've also been told that I have pretty damn good intuition."

That seemed to spark Connor's interest. He pulled at his other earlobe.

"Oh yeah? What does your intuition tell you about me, then?"

"That you seem like a nice enough guy."

Connor moistened his lips, which quivered with what I suspected was amusement, as he sat with his legs wide apart.

"And?"

"And you're fishing for compliments that I'm not going to give you just yet."

Connor threw his head back, indulging in a belly laugh. The rich, throaty sound filled me with pleasure. A smile that I couldn't suppress burst through.

"That's a fair call, Gypsy, fair call."

The silence was a comfortable one, our shared joke establishing the early threads of friendship. He looked at me. "What exactly do you mean by intuition? Like common sense? Women's intuition is usually pretty sharp."

He'd found me out. My abilities were stronger as a child, but I'd turned them off after the night that I told my father about the old woman in their bedroom, who was mystified by our presence and asking us to leave her home. They had looked up the records and it turned out that she died there. The expression on his face and the change in his tone of voice reinforced my revelation that talking with the dead was not a good thing. At puberty, the whole psychic telepath deal resurfaced with a vengeance, but it still felt wrong, the subject of ridicule. When my 'gift' or 'feyness' was proven with soon to be recovered fact, it was never mentioned. My parents' hushed whispers were intercepted through closed doors. Eventually, I figured out why mum called me Gypsy. My Romany grandmother had the gift, the second sight as well. One day, I'd ask if my name was a tribute or arranged as spite, but I still wasn't sure if I wanted to hear the answer. She spoke about my grandmother who died young as 'nervy' and 'fey' in a way that was both contemptuous and filled with longing.

The scrape of a chair on the floor brought me back to my surroundings. I wondered why I mentioned something like that to an almost stranger, albeit a hot one. I closed my eyes in the hope that a surge of courage and ease would overcome me. He seemed to be, if nothing else, a rare friend, carrying on from where we left off lifetimes ago.

"Well, I have some kind of…ability."

Connor's chin rested on one hand now, his attention riveted. "Go on…"

"Things happened to me as a girl. They freaked my parents out, scared them, so I switched them off. Er…they kind of …came back when I was a teenager."

"What kind of things? I bet you got a bit of attention back then, all sweet smiles and bright eyes." He reached up to tuck a lock of hair behind my ears and I sucked in a breath, as quietly and unobtrusively as I could.

Oh, God, this was embarrassing and amazing all at once. How the hell do I play this romance thing again?

Against my better judgment, I blushed. *Goddamn it.* Embarrassment, caused from not only the fact that my telepathic secret was out, but because of him, his attention…his *everything*. I couldn't think of anything more embarrassing than having my red face on display. Lost for words, I waited for my blistering cheeks to calm down a bit before continuing. However, Connor spoke first.

"It's okay, Gypsy. I'm not going to laugh at you, far from it." Connor leaned in with his elbows on the table, eyes never leaving mine.

Not only was he stunningly handsome, he seemed gentle. Then again, they all did at first. I wondered where the hell this seemingly perfect man came from. Maybe he was a dodo, the last of an extinct breed.

"I can talk to people without saying anything, without them even being in the same room. It took me a while to realize that most of them were …well, technically *dead*. The only living person I can 'speak' with is my niece, Renee. Definitely saves a lot of time and effort." I managed a hesitant smile as my gaze dropped to my heels. He was so startlingly good looking that I was nervous of him catching me staring. Like gobbling too much candy, it felt great, but was ultimately risky. *Please let this one be the one and not like my last failed relationship.* After four years, that one had broken my heart, and I'd later discovered he'd hooked up with a female friend of his bestie, Jack, within a month of our break up. He'd definitely moved on, although I'd struggled and remained single for ten months. I tried not to acknowledge that he'd possibly had both of us on a string.

Connor cleared his throat, bringing me back to the present. I decided to press on.

"These talks started early on as a child. Later on, I helped friends out with a few things, clearing ghosts from friend's places. You know, the classic ghost buster thing, and word started to spread. I can't just switch it on and off whenever I want to. It happens when it happens…"

"So you're a woman of many talents, then. You know, I've heard people say that before about this type of thing. It's not like a tap. I reckon there are plenty of us worried about family, wanting to be sure that they've moved on, are free of pain… I sure think about my brother…"

"You lost your brother? I'm sorry," I said.

"Yeah, my brother, Dan, died in an explosion. He was Aaron's dad and he also had a daughter, Christie. You might have heard it in the news, Melbourne courthouse. He was also part of the force." Connor brought a shaking hand to his forehead, his voice wavering slightly. "Rae, Dan's wife, never really got over it and the kids also took it pretty hard." Connor twisted the absent ring on his finger as he looked across at Aaron. "My wife, Jill, and I, took both of them in to live with us a year later. It was a bit rough at times, but what family doesn't have problems? Jill and I tried, but we could never have kids of our own." The skin bunched up around Connor's eyes, and one of his hands moved closer to Aaron before he quickly retrieved it. Aaron, who was nodding and tucking his hands behind his elbows, was having a rather stilted conversation with Matthew.

The waitress brought our meals over, silencing us. Connor had ordered a steak with all the trimmings, definitely a positive sign. A vegetarian could have been tedious.

After many delicious bites in an already comfortable silence, we took up where we left off.

"So, a detective," I said. "I haven't met one of those before. Have you been in the force for long?"

"Twelve years."

I wondered what twelve years in the force had been like and if he enjoyed his work.

He smiled slowly, but his shoulders slumped as he sagged back in the chair. "People ask me about the job and if it was a deliberate choice. I'm not sure what the short answer to that is. Some people say it's a duty, and that is part of it. It's not glamorous, with far too much paperwork for that. You see people at their worst, which was a bit of a shock in the early days. After that, I've never been surprised by what people do. On bad days, I tell myself I'm giving victims a voice."

His smile wavered as he waited for my reply, but for my part, I'd finished talking. I wanted to savor the chance to look at him under the pretense of listening intently.

"Most people seem to think it's like the cop

shows, with the adrenaline rush of the investigation and kicking in doors, but I can't remember how many times I've been beaten up, kicked, spat on, and shot at."

"Sounds like you should write a book."

"Yeah, I've heard that before. I'm not interested, plus, I can't write to save my life. Too busy doing what I do, I guess." He poked at a slight indentation in the wooden table.

A clang of glasses and a smash diverted all eyes to the bar, where a pretty, red-faced waitress smiled sheepishly. I looked across to see Aaron shaking Matt's hand firmly. Aaron must have taken the handshake as his cue to leave. As he leaned to speak with his uncle, I got a whiff of something metallic and dusty, probably from the construction site he worked at.

"Sorry, but I'm going to have to go. Early start tomorrow and it's been a big day." Connor slammed his hand into his nephew's with a jerk.

Was Aaron's look questioning or a challenge?

Connor released his grip and moved his chair back across the floor.

"No problem, thanks for coming. Talk to you soon, buddy." With a scrape of the chair, Aaron stood up and clumsily half-raised a hand in goodbye.

"Nice to meet you," I said, waving my hand, and with that, he was gone.

"Gypsy, I could talk to you all night, but…" Connor grinned so wide that his eyes narrowed, and he winked at me, "I better catch up with Matt for a bit, or he might get offended. Maybe when you're in the area next, we could catch up for a coffee?" He pulled a card from his wallet and laid it on the table.

A tingling sensation seized my chest and a tiny bead of sweat trickled down my back. I wasn't sure if it was the wine or a stupid crush, but it sure felt good. I couldn't remember the last time a man who took my fancy invited me out for coffee.

Connor had already moved to sit by Matt.

"Sounds good," I said.

The legs of my chair scraped as I moved to stand up. I went to stand with my back to the fire, feeling the warmth spread from my hands held behind me through the rest of my body.

Knowing Chloe and Rita, I was confident they wouldn't be able to resist rushing over to get the inside skinny. Sure enough, in less than a minute, they were by my side, searching my face like a couple of puppies waiting for a juicy tidbit to be thrown their way.

"Hey, Gyp, saw you got a business card. Geez, doesn't take you long, girl. Hope you wore matching undies tonight." Rita swigged down half a glass of wine in one gulp. Her narrow face was mocking me, as she rolled her eyes, set her wine glass on the shelf, and then pushed her hands out to warm them at the open fire.

"Piss off, Rita, jealousy makes you ugly." I lowered my chin to look at her, my feet apart in a fighting stance. Then, deciding to let it go, I turned to Chloe, who was struggling not to show her delight.

"Do you good to get a bit of action," she said. "Maybe there'll be less moaning. If you actually crack a smile at the next book club, I'll know why."

Chloe cackled and jabbed me with her elbow. I wished she wouldn't do that. My skinny frame doesn't do well when knocked, even in jest.

"Seriously," she continued, "I was hoping you'd come for this very reason. I'm glad you two hit it off."

"So this was a set up? For God's sake, Chloe, no wonder things started off so awkward. You could have warned me—even if he is gorgeous."

She glared at me as her hands flew in the air. "Come on, Gyp, lighten up. Haven't you heard the best thing for a break up is a rebound? It's been nearly a year since Mark, so it is time to get out and test the waters. Are you telling me that if there was a nice, warm, manly body like Connor's in bed that you'd kick him out? I doubt it." Smiling, Chloe placed her hand lightly on my shoulder.

My eyelids felt heavy and my energy was flagging. I was well past the nightclub era where I could stay out until dawn and bounce back for another eight hours of work.

"Well, girls, I wish I could say it's been a pleasure, but thanks to your matchmaking service, it was a tad uncomfortable." I crossed my arms and tapped my foot, before grinning, allowing my arms to fall.

"I have to admit, though, he's pretty damn charming and definitely a looker. It's quarter past ten, well past my bed time, so I'll be off now." I hitched up my purple Louis Vuitton bag, which had been hanging annoyingly around my elbow, and threw a fifty-dollar bill onto the table, watching as it wafted down. Before I left, I whispered in Chloe's ear, "Thanks, maybe, just maybe."

I gave a smile and a wave to Connor and Matt, promised Chloe I'd call her in a few days—which of course, she knew meant next month—and headed out the door. The smell of garlic and waves of laughter streamed behind me as the bell clanged its final goodbye. I turned off from the main drag, the satisfying clomp of my heels increasing my wine-imbued confidence, not to mention my happiness at a real life conversation with a hot looking someone of the opposite sex.

I passed the park gates, complemented with replica eighteenth century lamps that I admired every time I walked past them. I loved living in Carlton. It is the hub of the world and close to the iconic Lygon Street, lined with Italian restaurants as far as the eye can see, neon lights flashing, chairs and tables spilling onto the pavement. Couples can be seen hand in hand, too much in love to care about sales staff approaching them to enlighten them on their menu, while hot rods roar along with their horns blaring.

As I turned into a side street, my thoughts wandered. As I looked down the quiet residential street, lit softly by street lamps, I heard the rustling of wind in the trees and rattling of a rubbish bin in the dark alley to my left. It wasn't bin night, so it must be cats fighting or someone getting rid of some junk.

Wishing I'd remembered my glasses, I squinted as a commotion rose from further down the black laneway. There was a large van parked at the end and I could make out a figure loading something into it.

In that instant, I felt a wave of energy, something steely hard and terrifying. I could almost see it, like a slab of granite leading from the van directly to me. I'd learned the hard way not to deny my instinct, and so I took a quick detour into the alley. This wasn't the first time I'd acted in a mad rush of spontaneity. There was always the pepper spray in my bag if things got ugly. Besides, as my dad would say, no one would ever mug a woman like me. They would wait for someone else who was a lot less trouble. I was never sure whether to take that as a compliment or an insult, but at that moment, I didn't give a toss.

I cautiously stepped into the alley and became aware of the stillness. Not a soul was in sight. After a few steps, my foot struck an object in the dim shadows. As my eyes adjusted, I realized it was a rubbish bin, and a second later, it burst open with a clash.

I jumped and whimpered as a black shape streaked across the alleyway. A loud wail followed the cat as it sped off into the night. I waited for my heart to stop pounding in my ears, and for my body to stop trembling. Committed now, curiosity piqued and propelled by the terror rushing from the vehicle, I continued walking to the end of the isolated laneway wondering what was causing the terror.

I blew out a long breath, my feet continuing across on the cobblestones. Could the terror simply have been a cat?

As I got closer to the van, I saw what had been a hazy darkness, perhaps a couple of rubbish bags. Lying beside the open van door was a young woman lying on the ground. Someone must have tried loading her into the van unsuccessfully. Long, straw-colored hair fell across her face. Her wrists were tied and her mouth was gagged with duct tape. She was struggling to make some semblance of noise. Her long legs kicked like hell at the air. Her eyes were huge like saucers, reflecting the terror rolling off her in huge swells.

Something shifted in the blackness. As I tried to process what it was, it suddenly sprang from behind the van to offer me an up-close view. A man stood so near that his stinking, foul breath assaulted my senses. He towered over me in a dark hoodie, with his chest thrust forward, his elbows out. In the faint light of the streetlight in front of the alley, I could make out sandy hair. Other than that, his face was completely hidden by the head covering. His body carried a strange, unidentifiable smell, acrid and bitter.

I was supposed to be terrified, but instead, I felt shut off from reality, almost numb. I needed to grab the can of pepper spray from my bag, but I was paralyzed, rooted to the spot. Realizing that someone had summoned me, sent me a communication in desperation for me to intervene and ease their terror, the reality of the situation hit me. I set my shoulders and with head down slightly, I stared down the faceless bastard getting in my way.

"Fuck off, bitch..." he spat as I grabbed for my bag.

He seized the girl, shoving her into the back of the van roughly. I pitched forward to stop him, but he shoved me back with more force than I'd anticipated. I rocked back on my heels, hands flailing wildly, and as he slammed the van door closed, I just managed to stay upright.

My pulse was pumping madly, and the adrenaline had kicked in. I jumped at the sound of the engine starting. I ran for the front driver's window, which of course, he had locked, and started bashing it with my fists, screeching.

"Let her go! Let her *go*, you bastard!" I yelled so hard that a vein in my neck was pulsing and engorged.

I stood in front of the vehicle, legs planted wide part. I realized that the bastard could get away with this unless I identified him somehow. My eyes went down to the license plate. I reached into my handbag for my mobile phone, realizing I should have done this earlier and made a damn call to the cops.

He had gotten her into the van, but she wasn't going without a fight.

The woman had started banging with her feet, kicking the shit out of the van walls. I could almost see the outline of her foot bashing the thin metal veneer. With the key in the ignition, the man had turned up the radio to full blast, drowning out the noise of her screams and kicking.

The abductor revved the crap out of the van, the engine growling so loudly that I felt it through my toes. Nevertheless, I stood my ground, even with nails biting into my palms, pulse speeding, and heartbeat pounding. I'd get his details through to the police if it was the last thing I did.

I looked up to face him through the front window and the van launched at me. I dialed the emergency service number, holding the phone to my ear with fingers so rigid they hurt. The van came at me and in a split second, I was hit, my body bouncing off the van. My head took the brunt of the blow as I struck the brick wall, landing on the ground like a rag doll, unloved and discarded. Strangely, nothing hurt, at least, not at this moment, but I was sure that it should.

Colors of green, hot pink, and yellow, flashed. Tires squealed, and I thought I heard frantic footsteps approaching.

Then it was lights out.

*****

2

I jolted awake to the pungent smell of bleach and antiseptic curling its tendrils up through my nostrils and into my mind. My hands were clammy and my lips were trembling, my breath bursting in and out in loud gasps. I attempted to sit up, only to find the left side of my body glued to the bed. As I sank back down, the plastic mattress cover rustled.

Stretching my eyelids to their limit, I felt the right one give. The lid peeled apart slowly. This was usually the aftermath of a hangover, but usually the left one followed. Piercing sunlight lay on my right, perhaps a window. I couldn't see it, but I was pretty sure that was the source of the malicious light.

My stomach twisted as if it had been kicked, uneasiness at being in an unfamiliar room sending cool prickles over my clammy and sweaty skin. I squirmed in the bed. Had I been abducted? What happened to the girl last night? Was she alive? If so, then my kidnappers must be pretty damn tidy. Starchy, crisp sheets settled on my knees above and rubbed against the back of my legs. Lowering my chin, I caught a glimpse of heavy blankets, with clumsy lumps outlined beneath. It must mean my limbs were still attached. Some consolation, I guess.

Along the sterile white walls, I saw a sink, oxygen

mask, hazardous chemicals sign, and a dizzying array of other unidentifiable equipment. I laughed shakily, pressing a clammy palm to my chest, as I realized I was in a hospital. Thank God! Most likely, the doctors and nurses here would be of goodwill, although not always. I'd heard horror stories from friends with relatives who ended up in the hospital after car accidents, and ended up on a cocktail of psychiatric meds, becoming zombies beyond recognition. The theory would be tested soon enough when someone turned up.

A metallic slimy taste filled my mouth. I needed water desperately. I tried to swing my left arm across my body, but couldn't. Why the hell wouldn't my arm move? An everyday action I barely thought about and I couldn't bloody well do it. I tried the right arm and it lifted as if feather light, bringing a surge of relief. At least something worked. From outside the door came hushed voices and the quiet scuffle of what I could only assume were nurses' shoes.

I tried to speak. A pathetic parting of the lips ensued and no words came out at all, nothing but a slimy trail of spittle. I wiped it away with the back of the only wrist I could move, the hand scratching at my face on the way down. I couldn't speak. Oh, my God, how could this be happening? I shook my head and tried scooting my backside back up the bed to get into a higher position and watch what was happening. My attempt was in vain. I needed to be in control to some degree, but I wasn't sure about my chances at the moment, although my dogged persistence had served me pretty well, up to that point. I wished I was up to screaming, but I felt so groggy and slow that it was totally beyond me. Instead, I keened silently within my head. This was too much, all too much. It couldn't be happening.

At least, I could still feel. Surely, someone knew what was going on? I reached across with my right hand, managing to get my fingers curled around some type of remote. Then I threw it at the wall, where it sailed through the air, landing with an almighty crunch on the door before falling to the floor with a clatter. That should get someone's attention. I struggled to wrap the fingers of my right hand around the edge of the mattress, my limbs jerking as I struggled to move. How could it be that no one heard me? As the sound of a nurse's shoes increased from barely there to audible, and then just to outside the room, I realized I'd attracted the desired attention. It was time for some answers. The door opened and there they were.

"You're awake. Good, that means we won't have to wake you up later to take your blood pressure," said a brown-haired, olive-skinned nurse. She padded around to my right to pat my leg. Another woman with red hair, freckled skin, and the same light blue uniform followed. In her case, the uniform was stretched as far as it could across her folds and rolls.

"Gypsy, your friends were here while you were in surgery," said the redhead. "Emergency services traced your call and the ambulance brought you in. The police will want to interview you soon. A report has been filed, but you don't need to worry about that now. Let's get you better first."

My shoulders rounded, and I pulled the sheet up to cover myself. I shook my head and pointed at my mouth. I couldn't speak and didn't want to talk to police yet. I needed a day or so to recover at least.

I was frustrated. Not remembering fully how I'd ended up here, I glanced at the redhead, while curling my fingers to smooth my hair back.

I wanted to know who the nurses were, what they knew, and when they were going to let me out of the hospital.

I wondered if they were going to tell me their name.

As if on cue, the nurse on the right piped up.

"I'm Tina, and this is Colleen. We'll talk to the police for now if you like, delay them for a bit, but I'm sure they'll be back tomorrow, because they're keen to interview you. We'll be looking after you today."

I nodded my head slightly, thankful. I wondered how this whole interchange would go. The nurses were talking at me as if I wasn't there at all.

Hello, can we focus on the patient here for just a sec?

I'd worked out which one was good-cop and which was bad-cop. I hoped that Colleen wasn't planning on giving me a sponge bath, if they even did sponge baths anymore. Frowning, I pushed my feet down to the footboard at the bottom of the bed with a pleasing bang. That should get the message across, no sponge bath for me. I clutched at the sheets, feeling the clinical, starchy texture.

Tina touched my forearm, sending a jolt through me, which hit my forehead with a zap. Pinging pictures pushed their way in at the speed of light. I saw an overweight, balding man, sitting on an armchair and turning away. A feeling of unbearable sadness accompanied glorious pictures of a newborn baby, with Tina looking on in awe. Split second collages, so many pictures, coming at me so fast that I almost couldn't keep up. A white car smashed up accordion like, a huge gathering in black, coffin lowering into the ground, Tina collapsing inconsolable at the graveside.

"Can you move your fingers for me, honey?"

A rubber band snapped me back into the present and the connection was broken.

I wriggled my fingers, and as I bent my right arm up at the elbow, a smirk moved across my face. If I were able, I would have screamed my excitement down the corridors. However, all I managed was a lopsided grin from the right side of my mouth; complete with drool, which I hoped wasn't oozing all the way down my chin. I wiped my damp lips with the back of my hand. When Tina handed me a tissue, I managed to grunt out something resembling a thank you.

"Your friends said you ventured into a dark alley on Saturday night. Why would you do that?"

"Colleen…" Tina began with a warning tone.

Tina was still touching my arm, so if she was a receiver, she'd get my thoughts and the messages I was sending her. I was hoping she was the exception, and had the antennae like Renee. Some people—not many living ones, anyway—got my thoughts, and it didn't take long at all. In fact, with Renee, it was almost instant. Not everyone could do it, though. It depended on where their awareness frequency was set, and which station they were tuned into.

"Right. Better get on with checking your vital signs then. I can see a slight droop on your left side, Gypsy, so it is possible that the brain injury has affected your movement there and possibly your speech. You were lucky. You have multiple injuries. The doctor will be in soon to discuss your treatment options."

Sweat gathered under my eyes, and my right hand was clenched into a fist. I tried to signal how I felt by pursing my bottom lip and blowing my hair out of my face. What did they mean anyway, brain injury? What brain injury? Is that what happened to me? I wished Tina could share my thoughts. I had so much to tell her if I could just shake off the slowness.

I felt like I was underwater. My head reeled so badly that I wondered if it was moving.

Tina was sliding the blood pressure cuff off. She patted me gently.

"The doctor will be in to see you soon."

I pointed at Tina, trying to get her attention. I needed more information, but she had already padded away along with Colleen. Now I fully understood how a swimmer felt struggling underneath the water. My limbs moved at a snail's pace and the pea soup fog in my head was thick. Maybe, just maybe, this was all a dream. One of those nightmares where I couldn't move fast enough to escape the monster would be good about now. I could wake up in my bed at home, shake the whole mess off, and get on with the business of living.

My eyelids were like lead and I struggled to keep them open. I needed to stay awake as long as possible. There was work to be done. I needed to get well so that I could not only report what I saw, but investigate further. Must. Stay. Awake. Must…

The room faded as I succumbed to the wash of lead haze and I drifted off.

*****

As Connor switched off the alarm, he knew it was going to be a rough one. The rumor mill was already in overdrive, and his phone had notified him with a ping.

A young woman, a police headquarters employee had gone missing last night.

The kicker was the confidential reports she'd swiped on the way out of the building. Reports about suspected crooked cops, written by internal affairs and for the eyes of that department only. Seems this lady was curious and not all she appeared to be.

He'd been exhausted last night and needed a full night's sleep. It was still dark outside as he slid out of bed and slipped on his running gear. His morning run helped him keep his thoughts straight and make a reasonable start to the day. He grabbed his water bottle from the shelf beside the door, and headed outside. If he didn't run, he'd go insane, or at least more insane than he felt already, dealing with the unrelenting pressure of being senior detective. As he headed down the steps, he heard the satisfying clunk of the door closing.

Cold air stung his skin, and his breath formed plumes of mist that streamed past his eyes. Lengthening his stride, Connor pulled the iPod from his pocket to clip it onto his waistband. Some cops turned to drink, some to drugs, and others went off the rails. After the failure of his marriage, he had turned to running, three miles a day.

The rhythm of his feet hitting the pavement reassured him, guiding him on. As Connor's thoughts turned to the woman he'd met at dinner the night before, excitement prickled along his shoulders and the backs of his arms. Damn, she was hot, not what he'd expected. He thought she'd be some annoying breathless woman giggling with nerves. She was not only gorgeous, but had a keen intelligence, and her feistiness was appealing. Matt had mentioned that "a friend of a friend who's single" would be there, but Connor had been so focused on current cases, some of which were getting intense, and the conflicting demands of the bureaucratic bunglers at head office that when he'd met Gypsy, it was almost a physical sensation, a jolt he'd definitely not been expecting.

She wasn't like the fleeting presence the others had been. Something about the way she looked at Connor made him sure she understood and wanted to get to know him. There were so many things he wanted to share with her, but he couldn't. No way in hell. Some things, including the years of IVF, the needles, the expense, and the resentments that built up eventually to crack his marriage were too raw, too private to share with anyone.

He thought about their conversation, the fact that Gypsy had never met a detective.

The day he'd made detective was etched in his memory. Back then, they didn't have a clothing allowance, so polyester shirts with mismatched pants had to make do. The day he got his Ford Falcon, the car of his dreams, Connor had stood with chest out, a proud gleam in his eye. Sure, it wasn't the most modern vehicle ever, but it was unmarked and it was his. He polished it and cleaned it to within an inch of its life. He carted the bare essentials along in the boot: a fishing tackle box filled with a fingerprinting kit, crime scene tape, extra ammo, paper towels, a spare expandable baton, and a Smith and Wesson model ten revolver, which replaced the new issue pistol some time ago. His M&P 40 semi-automatic pistol rarely left his nylon belt, along with the Hiatts handcuffs and the spare Motorola tactical radio with hand piece.

He wasn't prepared for the loneliness and alienation of his new lot in life. The sheer workload and often twenty-hour days only added to the pressure of fighting with his wife about IVF treatments. Jill screamed that he was never there when she needed him, and he brought his head down slightly. He knew it was true. In a bid to connect, gain reassurance that at least some of his colleagues would understand, Connor had turned to his former workmates, but the camaraderie he'd enjoyed with his fellow boys in blue was a thing of the past.

He wanted to tell Gypsy how it had been back in the Drug Squad when he was still feeling his way around in his detective's skin. Connor held his head high, remembering the jealousy of his brothers. He had also changed over the years, and the superiority complex he swore he'd never have had slowly shifted his view of the world. He remembered how it felt to spend hours sitting in the woods watching suspects, with mosquitos sucking the blood from him relentlessly, along with occasional visits from spiders and snakes. Not to mention the unrelenting rain and snow.

Nobody had told him how it would feel to work undercover, especially when walking into the middle of a drug deal unarmed. His training hadn't prepared him for how it felt when his cover was broken. The shock of being shot at, spat on, beat up, kicked, scratched, stabbed, cut, knocked down, punched, and pepper sprayed with his own spray, all while wearing a suit. How it felt to kill a man, even one that was practically begging him to do it, a once in a lifetime experience. The way the nineteen-year-old armed robber had hidden behind a car, popping his head out repeatedly, a sitting duck. He'd held back knowing this was the case and that the guy was obviously under the influence of drugs, and wanted to be shot. Why else would he come out from the car and wait like that with a smile and a nod? How the young man's face would stay with him forever, and so would the look on the parents' faces as Connor broke the news to them.

He wanted to tell Gypsy all of these things, but couldn't find the strength to do it. Besides, technically, he hardly knew her. He poked his tongue inside his cheek, realizing without a shadow of a doubt that he damn well couldn't tell her that he and Jill had split up because of the strain of being infertile. The treatments over the years, and all the baggage of IVF, and for all that, the problem was with Jill. He had already fathered a child.

When he had just turned eighteen, he spent most of his time at the home of his older brother, Dan, and his young wife, Rae. He idolized Dan and found himself drawn to him, every word and deed a revelation. He'd mimicked him in every way he could, even becoming a police officer just like him.

One afternoon, when Aaron was at daycare, Rae had confided in him about the trouble in her marriage: Dan's long hours, her intense loneliness. Crying, she apologized for burdening him at such a young age. Connor didn't care. He was just glad that someone actually trusted him enough to spill their guts, and he'd held her tightly as the sobs wracked her body. It had seemed only natural that they had ended up in bed together. He'd never forgotten it, what eighteen-year old would? It was his first sexual experience, not that he ever would have told his mates in the final year of school. Anyway, it was private, something for him to hold onto and savor. He wasn't the type that bragged to his mates, so he'd kept it to himself, reliving the encounter night after night, smiling a smile as he carried his secret, which only made the experience more monumental.

When he heard that Rae was pregnant, and Christie arrived nine months later, Connor had been terrified. At once, he stopped visiting so often. Dan had asked what was going on, but Connor simply shrugged, playing the angst-ridden teenager card. Over the years, he noticed the similarities that he and his niece shared, but kept quiet, desperately hoping no one else saw it.

He also wouldn't be confiding in Gypsy about the one-night stands, the women that had approached him once they'd discovered he was available. It was as if someone had turned on a magnet or a switch, announcing a married man suddenly separated. He wondered if they felt sorry for him. The pretty blonde journalist and the red headed constable he'd slept with since his split with Jill had comforted him, their warm bodies filling the loneliness temporarily. He hadn't wanted any more than that, and they knew it, or he hoped they did. He'd told them and they nodded and smiled but he wondered. Wondered if they were simply responding as he'd expected them to, remaining hopeful. Thankfully, the journalist wasn't loose-lipped. Connor wouldn't have been able to stand the pity or the congratulatory slaps on the back down at the station.

He set his jaw and pushed his shoulders back. He

would never be able to tell Gypsy, although, maybe someday he would want to. Some things were better left unsaid. Although she seemed approachable, saying them out loud would make them more real and solid, and he wasn't sure if he was ready for that. It was still early days. He looked forward to getting to know her. He smiled to himself, hoping she would get in touch. Women could be coy about that sort of thing, but in her case, he had a feeling he just might get a phone call.

*****

A base drum pounded inside my skull, forming cracks in my vision. I opened my eyes to slits and looked around. The hospital room was now dimmed to a grey hue, thanks to some sympathetic soul who had closed the blinds. I felt more alert, not as badly off my face with God knows what medical drugs. As my gaze moved from the window to the chair, I saw Leah perched precariously on the edge of the seat. Her skin was pale and translucent, her short brown hair tousled. I sucked in a quick breath and shook my head, feeling the blood rush to my face. For the first time in a long while, I wondered if she really did care.

Her dark hair was just as wild as it had always been, and her mouth was still set in a grimace, accepting all that was barely tolerable. If Leah and I had spent our lives in a squabble of a half-lived life, her daughter Renee was my primary hope that some people may turn out to be half-decent. Her first words as a toddler had been "Nay," pointing to herself with a chubby sausage finger, and "Arny Gyp." Over the years, the names had stuck, and she didn't seem to mind being called Nay or horse-face. Meanwhile, I accepted that I was Arny Gyp, depending on how she felt. At the age of thirteen, she'd become a seriously studious, yet, an angelically beautiful child.

I grabbed the side of the mattress in an attempt to leverage my body up, which failed miserably. My hand bobbed as I searched for the bed remote. My fingers, finally making contact, curled around its plastic edges and soon the bed sighed with an electric hum, as it, and my back, began their upward journey. I felt a lot more civilized in the upright position, more able to cause an effect and almost ready to face the day, although the drugs wearing off probably had more to do with that. The base drum in my head shifted from the right to the left, and I flinched as it pounded with greater intensity. Shame I didn't want any painkillers, but I needed to be alert and awake.

"Gyp," said Renee, her neck bent as she came out from behind her mother's chair to walk toward me, hands brushing across various objects of the room, the window ledge, the end of the bed, feeling her way. She dragged her feet over to my bedside and reached gently to feather her fingers across the scar on my head. Rocking slightly, her hands continued in a gentle exploratory gesture over my shaved scalp. Her right hand slid away, moving to her throat where she clutched at her locket. Warm moisture tickled the corner of my eye. Her simple gesture was so innocent, no need to pretend. I didn't bother raising my right arm to stop her.

"You're okay, you're okay." Her eyes were furrowed, an expression out of place on such a beautiful young face.

I sighed, wishing I could talk to her, and hear my voice again; a luxury lost to me which I hoped was temporary. I raised my one good hand off the bed, only for it to fall back exhausted by the effort.

"You collapsed and I heard the nurses say your brain bled. I'm so glad you're still around, Gyp."

I was pretty damn glad I was alive, too, even if at that moment, I couldn't speak. I knew that Nay of all people would understand. I opened my mouth in my second attempt, resulting in not only the expected spittle launch, but also a groan, which sounded very close to *Nay*, although it also resembled the bray of a calving bovine. Regardless, I decided to take it as progress. Snatching at the tissues on the table, I managed to form my fist around a few before knocking the box to the floor.

"Did you just try to say my name, Gyp? Did you?"

I stretched out my hand to her again and she looked at it, biting her lip. She picked up the box and pushed it back onto the bedside table, but even as she did, her eyes went towards the exit. I willed her with every ounce of energy I had left to take my hand, so I could feel human again.

She placed her young hand underneath mine, and I felt the soft, warm deliciousness nestling there. I saw her pictures, as I'd done so many times before. This was our shared secret, the unspoken agreement that we would never give to Leah, who we knew would be jealous, a power line cursing through us at electric speed. I felt Renee's energy, the buzzing of the force field that kept her alive.

Nay's smile wavered as I saw her at school, sitting despondent on a bottle green wooden bench, the paint peeling and chipped at the edges, her half unpacked lunch box beside her. She pulled out a biscuit and nibbled on it nervously, gazing across the playground at a gaggle of children running, chasing, screaming and climbing. Her attention was fixed on a golden haired boy, tall and laughing, who looked over at her sitting alone. He scampered over, intoning nasally "Renay-y, Renay-y, bad breath spray-y." As he ran away, I felt her loneliness.

What's going on?

She looked at me and rolled her drooping shoulders, twisting her neck as if sore.

Now it was my turn and I showed her my pictures, the cinema reel of Saturday night. Aware there were two of us in the picture, her presence was with me as I relived it all, her chest caving, feet shuffling, and fingers pulling at the collar of her school dress. I showed her my night out, chatting to my book club friends, meeting Connor, warming myself by the fire. She looked on as I left the restaurant, walked past the park, stumbled upon the young man in the alleyway, felt the terror of the young woman, confronting the faceless man loading his prey into the van, heard the squeal of tires, and felt the impact before collapsing.

Renee jerked her head back and touched her throat.

He hit you, Gyp, for real? He really hurt you—that's why you're here. That man wanted you dead. The van hit you hard. She took small steps closer, stroking my shoulder.

Her voice in my head confused me. Somehow, I'd blocked the head injury part out. I remembered the rest of the night so clearly: his outline in the semi-darkness, the terror rolling off the young woman in waves as she struggled to move, and then the shock of being rammed by the van. Yet, somehow, I'd always assumed that I'd collapsed from a stroke, not brain damage from being hit by a van – a one-off act, which was ridiculous. I mean, what are the odds of a stroke just minutes after stumbling across a crime?

Yet, Nay had been able to see what I couldn't or wouldn't. The blows from the van left me unconscious in a deserted alleyway as he sped away. The knuckles in my right hand cracked as I pounded my fist against the mattress. The bastard ran into me, so it was no wonder it hurt like hell. My head pounded again. My brain had bled and that man had left me for dead in the shadows, driving off with his prize. God only knew where he'd taken the young woman or what he had done to her from there. I shivered and muttered words indecipherable even to me. I spoke silently to Nay using our connection, my voice echoing inside her head.

Nay, this man is dangerous. You know what he did to that girl and me. You've heard his voice, and you know roughly his height and build. The police know about what happened when an ambulance was called—but there's one detective I want you to find urgently, Connor Reardon. Think of that woman's family and just imagine what they must be feeling right now.

Nay scratched her nose and bit the nails on her right hand. She knew most adults didn't listen to young kids. We both knew the police would more than likely laugh her off as some sort of wildly imaginative but cute preteen.

Why don't I take mum with me? That way, they won't write me off as a crazy, dumb kid.

She rested one hand beside me on the bed, and with the other, she stroked my cheek.

No, we don't need to involve your mum just yet. You know she'll panic. Trust me, I have a feeling Connor will be pleased to hear from you. Do this for me, please.

"I will, I promise I will." She nodded, her jaw set

firm.

"You okay, honey?" said Leah suddenly, straightening on the chair. At that moment, Renee and I realized she had spoken her promise out loud rather than thinking it.

My niece spun around on her back foot to face her mother, and I stared at the back of her school jumper covered in grey fluffy lint, willing her to turn back around.

Damn. I hoped she would end up at the police station and at least put it out there to establish the link with Connor. I knew it was a lot for anyone, let alone a thirteen year old, but she was strong. If anyone could give this a go, Nay could. I shook my head, pressing my lips together, feeling my throat closing up. I needed to get out of bed and get the investigation moving.

"No, Mum, of course not. I'm sad that Gyp's so sick. She looks different, that's all."

I squeezed Renee's hand, feeling the soft flesh encasing her bird-like bones and my back tingled as sweat formed. I sent her a final message.

Connor's business card might still be in my handbag, ask for him and only him.

Leah looked at her daughter sympathetically as Renee draped an arm around her shoulder.

"You're right, she does look different, honey," Leah murmured, her smile wavering, as she brushed Nay's fringe across her forehead. "The best thing we can do right now is be here and cheer her up as best we can."

I rolled my eyes as my gaze flicked upward. If I could have spoken at that moment, I would have yelled at Leah to give me a break, she was laying pretend concern on so thick that I needed to throw up in a sick bucket. When the hell was she ever there for me? The Mother Theresa act probably helped her to feel better, an ointment for her conscience, but all I wanted to do was gaze at the ceiling. Instead, I turned on one side with my hand tucked under my aching head, and yawned.

"Well, Gypsy, we're going to head off, I'm afraid. I know you're in good hands here and getting the best care available. We'll be back to see you in a couple of days." Leah picked up her handbag and faced the door, her mind already through it before she'd left.

My gaze was intense, refusing to break the connection with Renee as she followed her mother.

I hoped she'd come through and do what I'd asked of her. Maybe later, she could tell me all about her adventure at the police station.

With that, they were gone.

*****

3

The bell rang out and as the children spilled out of the classroom, Renee dragged herself out to the peg on the corridor wall where her bag hung, waiting to be taken home.

Today was the day, and she wasn't looking forward to it. She had promised Gyp she would tell the police everything she knew. Her head dropped and she swallowed hard. She wondered if her aunt had powers that could undo things so Renee didn't have to know everything, but somehow she doubted it.

Renee wondered if this was what being electrified felt like. The sour taste in her mouth, the ache in the back of her throat and the weight in her chest suggested that just might be what was happening.

Usually, as she headed out into the sunshine, she savored the rays warming her face, but today, she wished time would speed up, as she opened the squeaky school gate and headed out along Louis Street.

The cop shop was on the way home off Laine Road. She knew the route home by heart, walking past the police building each day, each grudging footstep bringing her closer to the duty she had felt weighing her down all day.

She could already see the condescending smiles.

With her, most adults adopted a patronizing tone as if talking to the village idiot. Renee got it. She knew she was "just a child" no matter how much she instinctively understood. From an early age, she could detect emotional nuances, other people's delight and distress. However, experience had taught her not to let on that she understood completely their problems and conflicts when talking to adults, or she would suffer the consequences of rude jibes and condescending pats on the head. There were some things they were keen to hold on to, like the idea that only they understood rivalries and petty jealousies, and they became very upset when a child understood and thought exactly as they did.

Gyp was the best, not just because they got along so well, but also because she was the only one who spoke to Renee as an adult. Of course, the subject of Gyp's abilities came up in those conversations, especially when Renee started manifesting these skills as a child. Bringing her head close to her blonde head, her aunt had confided in her, sharing her experiences and passing on what little information she had about her grandmother, Renee's great grandmother, and how hard it must have been for her, too. Renee's eyes filled with tears, and she wiped them away quickly, imagining her great grandmother beside her and Gypsy, and guiding them both on. Somehow, the idea of ancestors shaping their destiny reassured her.

She didn't remember a time when they'd agreed not to tell her mum about their little secret; it was implied. Then again, since Dad left, Mum spent most of her time worrying about bills and money, grey smears growing under her eyes from exhaustion. Renee heard her sobs late at night, the cries seeping through the walls. She didn't want to burden her mother more than necessary, and lately, Gyp had been the sounding board she needed.

Renee stopped abruptly at the entranceway and her stomach curled with even greater intensity. She'd never really paid attention to the local police station, but today, she looked with glazed eyes at the stone steps with the brightly lit blue police sign with white text above, announcing her destination.

With a sigh and a heave of her shoulders, Renee climbed to the glass door. She pushed it open and headed into the hushed lobby. Fluorescent lights, blue plastic chairs nailed to the linoleum waiting room floor, notices hanging by a thread on the board and a desk immediately in front of her, complete with one-way mirrors, only added to her fear that all eyes were on her. She patted her hair and pulled her jacket tighter.

She plonked her school bag on the ground, where it landed with a loud *whack*, and she waited, her feet tapping on the linoleum. A door to the right of the mirrored wall opened and a young man emerged, his dark hair thick. He wore a light blue uniform. He stood looking at her, the question across his face before he asked it.

"Can I help you?"

In the mirror, Renee saw herself flush crimson as the floor rushed up to meet her. She prayed she wouldn't faint.

"Er…Officer, is Connor Reardon here? I want to report a crime."

"Okay, and what would be the nature of this crime?"

"Well, an attack. An…ah…" Renee began.

"Does your mum and dad know about this?"

She twisted the sleeve of her school jumper, her gaze jumping from the officer to the exit behind her. She'd told Gyp she wouldn't be taken seriously, but her aunt had been determined. This was a really stupid idea.

"Well, you see, it's…confidential."

The officer looked down at her, his mouth set in an unwavering line. "Confidential?"

"I'd rather not tell Mum about it just yet."

The police constable pressed his lips together. "I see. Just a minute, I'm just going to get some more information. Won't be long." He disappeared out of the same door he'd come in, going to the mysterious offices beyond.

What?

Renee wondered what he thought of her. Eventually, the sliding doors granted entry to a man who stood behind her forming a queue. He looked as though he belonged here.

This was a bad idea. I shouldn't have come. What on earth was Gyp thinking?

Gypsy and an unknown woman lying helpless or dead somewhere in the middle of nowhere. Was this really worth it?

Sighing, Renee picked up her bag, toying with the idea of sprinting to the street below, when a different man emerged from the mysterious back office to plant his body at the front desk.

Something about him seemed less intimidating, almost friendly. Maybe it was his blond hair, rounded shoulders. His squinting eyes lit up with an inner glow, and he had a tentative smile and laugh lines around his eyes. When he dropped his pen, saying, "Oops," that sealed the deal. She decided she would take the plunge and tell him everything. She just hoped Gypsy was right and that he would prove himself trustworthy.

"I hear you need to report something confidentially, is that right? The constable said you asked for me by name," he said and leaned forward with a smile.

"Yes, that's right."

"Why don't we talk in the room over here then? How does that sound?" He glanced at the official looking person waiting patiently behind her, and gestured behind him with a pointed finger signaling that another officer would be out in a minute.

"Um, okay, I guess we could do that."

Renee read the tag pinned to his shirt – Det. Constable Reardon - and followed him through a gate to her left. At the threshold to the dimmer room, she stood unmoving. The lights were doing their best, but the blue, windowless room with scuffed skirting, shabby chairs, and rickety table had an air of desolation. Renee pictured her mother with the phone to her ear in the hallway at home, greyish pallor spreading as she learned that her daughter was at the police station. She imagined the conversation: that she was assisting with their enquiries into an abduction and possible murder. Considering Leah's fragile state since Dad's departure, this would be the catalyst that would drop Leah from hanging over the precipice to a terrifying freefall into the abyss.

"Excuse me? Is everything all right?" Connor asked, his head up.

"Ah…yes, sorry." Returning to reality, Renee shuffled across to the plastic seat at the wobbly table.

Detective Reardon leaned back in his chair as he

rested his pen and paper on the table

"Were you referred to me? How can I help?" He said it with kindness in his voice and Renee nodded.

"Yes, I was. My Aunt Gypsy told me to come and find you. She met you last Saturday night at dinner. She's sick and is in the hospital, she's hurt."

His eyes were wide and unblinking.

"Gypsy Shields? I remember her, what happened?"

"She's in the hospital. She had a bleed on the brain. On the way home from the restaurant, someone drove into her and then left."

"Oh, I see." He rubbed his chin, leaning back in his chair. "How badly is she hurt?"

Renee fiddled with the hem on her school uniform, wishing she was back in the sanctuary of the quiet classroom. She didn't want to think about her aunt lying in the hospital after surgery. It was too much.

"She can't talk right now and can only move one side. The nurses said she had a brain bleed and she has nasty, purple-black bruises. She was walking home when she heard something down a dark alley. At first, she thought it was a couple of cats fighting, and as she got closer, she thought maybe it was a man and woman…" she blushed, "…you know. Then she realized it was a man standing over a woman, who was trying to scream but her mouth was covered over and she was tied up. Gyp was so terrified that she couldn't move, but later, when she tried to stop him, he ran her over with his van."

Detective Reardon gripped the pen tightly, bouncing his foot on the floor. His gaze darted toward the window.

"I see. You're aware of her abilities then? She

shared them with you?" Detective Reardon asked, with his eyebrows raised.

Here we go, she thought; the laughter or the embarrassed strained silence, or even a sudden intense interest in floor particles.

"Well…yes, I guess so." She raised her head ever so slightly, the curtain of her hair shielding her.

The frown was still deeply etched into his forehead as he met her gaze. Maybe, just maybe, he was a friend, an ally who would know what to do.

"It's okay, truly." His tone was gentle. "We need to find out who did this. Thank you for finding me. I appreciate it and so does your aunt."

Renee felt a prickle of tears at her eyes. To force them back, she focused on the table, taking deep breaths. "Yes, Gypsy and I have an understanding." There, she'd said it. It hung heavy in the air, a balloon rising slowly towards the flickering light.

He tapped his fingertips together, forming a steeple. "You mean like telepathy? Its okay, Gypsy explained to me what she does. I'm not going to laugh at you or her, far from it."

"Well, she hates that word. She says there are too many wackos about. She does what she does to help people, not for money. It might seem funny, but she can tune into people pretty well."

In that instant, she saw the safety of talking to him so clearly. He wasn't doubled over in laughter, pointing fingers as he howled at the ridiculousness of what she'd put to him. He was rubbing at his chin again, looking at her intently.

"This is a pretty serious incident. I'll take down your and your aunt's details and get moving on this straight away. At the moment, we're getting a lot of calls to the Crime Stopper line. Some more pressing than others. This might be what we need to solve the case."

Renee smiled slowly, standing up on wobbly legs. He'd help them, just like Gypsy said. No wonder she liked him. Of course, Renee was a child, and wasn't supposed to be aware of adult mechanisms, but there it was. His kindly concern was probably tied in with his interest in her aunt.

"So, can I tell Gypsy you'll come by to see her? She was pretty insistent that I tell you about this."

"Of course you can. Which hospital is she in?"

She parroted off the hospital ward and bed number, Renee's home address and the phone number. Renee hoped he'd interview her aunt in the hospital when her Mum was there so she could explain things in a more public place, rather than Mum having a meltdown from the worry. She still wondered if he might be humoring her and would turn out to be a no show, but she hoped not.

After the relief of her task fulfilled, she felt the blood rush back to her chest. Her chair scraped as she pushed it under the table.

"Thank you for listening to me, Detective Constable Reardon." She looped the final strap of the backpack over her shoulder. "I better get going, because I really don't want Mum to worry too much."

He nodded thanks, and walked her back to the sliding door.

*****

Connor Reardon punched in the security code to head back to the cubicle, slapping paperwork on his desk as he sagged in the chair. This case had become a damn minefield. Not so much investigation wise, since after twelve years, he'd mapped his own course. However, politically, he knew the shit storm was brewing due to the confidential paperwork Joanne Seyers, the administrator, had taken with her the night she went missing. The powers that be were bracing themselves for the media blitz sure to detonate in a case where a pretty young blonde employee of Victoria Police, suddenly disappeared.

He already suspected how this one would play out. A missing woman, police following up leads with no evidence, overall failure to find a perpetrator, all offering maximum fodder for journalists. The brass would be nervous, particularly as the information in the reports described senior detectives relocating the proceeds of crime, cash, drugs, and weapons. The chief would be in a particularly foul mood, and most of the personnel were giving him a wide berth, Connor included.

Since the call went out for all suspicious activity to be reported to Crime Stoppers, no matter how insignificant, the team had sifted through the weird and wonderful as par for the course. Something about the solemnity of this child told Connor there just might be a genuine lead at the end of a long and winding road. He'd go past the hospital soon. He wanted to see Gypsy again. He remembered the way she looked at him when he spoke, listening intently like he was the only person in the world. He couldn't remember the last time someone had made him feel that way: important, interesting, and dare he say it, attractive.

He decided to see her after his shift finished around eight o'clock tonight. It couldn't hurt and he really wanted to see her again. In addition, he needed to interview her. He wanted to find the bastard that hurt her.

4

His heart rate had subsided. He hadn't planned this one. Aaron had known he'd find the perfect girl soon, someone to love and adore him, no questions asked. When he saw her, he knew at that moment that he would take her to a new life. The monumental fight with Tiran still rang in his ears. He stormed out for a drive, a pressure cooker needing to let off steam. When he saw her after that boring fucking dinner, conditions were perfect. He looked ahead, the white lines on the road a beacon in the darkness guiding him to his destination. He'd told her it would be easier on both of them if she kept quiet, and he wouldn't kill her. However, she wouldn't listen, so he swung the steering wheel to veer across to pull over, her screams piercing his brain. She wouldn't stop, even with the tape across her mouth, so he'd rolled up his sleeves. Frustrated, he'd swung the van door open and he'd yelled at her to shut up, which of course, she wouldn't do, so he'd been forced to beat her with the crowbar until she went quiet.

He had thought she would be different, not like the others, her pure, soft skin and perfect face tantalizing, luring him into a tangled web. His body tensed as he thought about that stupid cow that got in his way earlier. If she hadn't shown her ugly face, he could have shown his new lady some love, shown her how good he could be. As he bent over the steering wheel, he grimaced, spittle building up in the corners of his mouth. The muscles in his face were twitching. He had gotten impatient, which was his first mistake, and his last. It didn't matter. Things would still turn out fine. He was sure of it. He was on the way to Pop's place and as soon as he arrived, he could relax and they could settle into their home. It was the perfect base to start a new family.

Things had started so well when he'd met Tiran. Now here they were three years later, caught in the routine of nappies and work, the constant nagging giving him a headache. He'd thought she understood him. They seemed to have so much in common, making a united front, them against the world. When his son had come along ten months ago, things had taken a turn for the worse. He could feel himself fading away to a shadow, invisible, nothing of his former self was left. Tiran didn't seem to want him near her anymore. The baby was the center of her world, the bond between them so strong he knew he was useless, no longer needed or wanted. When he climbed into bed at night, there was literally no room for him. She was feeding the baby, sprawled out across the mattress, staking her claim. She looked at him with scorn and he'd snorted off in a huff to sleep in the spare room.

On Saturday, it had all come to a head. After the heated screaming match, her fingers pointing at him, accusing him, as if reaching inside his head slowly to burn, he knew he'd needed to get out of there fast before he burst a fuse, so he packed a bag and high tailed it. On the way out, he'd shoved her, a gentle push he'd thought. It wasn't planned, and she'd fallen and hit her face on the coffee table on the way down. Holding his head in his hands, he told himself it was her fault, she wouldn't leave him alone, and she knew his limits but pressed on regardless. She just wouldn't leave things alone. He'd told her that, his shoulders curling over his chest, and it wasn't as if she hadn't been warned.

Saturday night, he headed out to dinner and on the way home, he saw Cinderella walking along Lygon Street. Feeling pulled into her trail, as if a magnet was drawing him in, he had no choice but to follow her. She was alone, blonde, and beautiful. Something about the way she flicked her hair back, sending the light shining, before turning into a side street, left him silent with wonder. She'd looked over her shoulder as she turned, the gesture encouraging him. She was seeking him out. They would start a family together, him, her, and Bailey, a fresh start. He knew it, and he could relax and enjoy the life he deserved. Once he had his new woman settled safely at the factory, he would go back and take care of business, and take his son where he belonged. He would tell Tiran he wanted to take Bailey out for a drive, give her some peace. He knew all women loved babies. All he would have to do is give the baby to Cinderella. She would be entranced and instantly know that he was hers and she was his. A new family and a brand new start was all they needed, and he deserved it more than most. This was his time.

*****

Today things seemed to be improving. Although

still confined in my grey hospital room, instead of my left limbs rolling off me like a rag doll, I had started to feel pins and needles in the lower part of my left leg, and could now feel some of the fingers on my hand. Even if the nurses told me these were phantom pains, I knew they weren't. Something was happening. Shit, any feeling was better than none, surely.

I'd started experimenting with pen and paper and was able to produce squiggly, but otherwise legible lettering. When you've been unable to speak for a couple of days, the ability to write *'get me the hell out of here'* is pretty damn thrilling.

Then there was my onward progress from the previous calving bovine attempt at speech with Nay. Restless, I'd exhaled, continuing my nasal intonations in a quieter tone. I still had some sense of dignity, and didn't want fellow patients or the nurses suspecting a thirty-year-old woman who hadn't had sex in a year, had defied nature and was miraculously giving birth to her first child. After a few groans, I managed to work out how to say simple things like look, here, no, and go, without sounding like I was giving birth. I felt a flutter in my belly, a floating sensation. I was expecting applause, as if I'd won a Nobel peace prize for dogged determination, when in reality, all I'd managed to do was enunciate words rather than squeaking, wailing or whimpering.

I was just scratching out a few more phrases in spidery text when Dr. Hyde sauntered in. Okay, maybe his name wasn't Dr. Hyde, but I'd had a brain bleed, for crying out loud, and a name that sounded like Nicaragua was well beyond me.

"Ms. Shields, we meet again," he said as he took the usual doctor-like pose, his hands inside his pockets, standing beside the bed I was resting in. I squinted up at him, his certainty projecting across the room as I picked imaginary fluff off my gown.

"Yes." I smiled hard, trying to hide the small jittery movements of my right hand and failing miserably. With my index finger, I wiped the sweat from my upper lip, quickly, and I hoped, unobtrusively.

"I must say, I'm impressed. Usually patients with a brain injury can spend weeks recovering their motor control and speech centers, but it seems your rehabilitation is ahead of schedule. I can quite confidently say that an effective rehabilitation program will certainly speed up your progress. Blood pressure is normal. There's been no further bleeding in the right lobe, no seizures, and I'm told you've had some slight sensation in your limbs." He grabbed the chart hanging at the bottom of my bed, flicking a page up and glancing at me with eyebrows raised in expectation.

"Yes," I said nodding. Stunning how my vocabulary was moving ahead in leaps in bounds.

Dr. Hyde took out his little hammer thing and the usual small silvery needle to deliver what would otherwise be an annoyance, but right now, was just what the patient ordered.

He blazed a trail across my left arm and leg. I flinched and managed to murmur a protest as he stabbed me very lightly with his needle. My skin formed goose bumps and I shied away from the stabs to my hand.

"Excellent," he said, patting his weapon in his pocket. "I'll definitely be recommending rehabilitation at the soonest possible opportunity and advise the team of today's developments. You're doing nicely,

Ms. Shields."

I went quiet, feigning interest in a magazine. I knew he couldn't resist that ever so subtly condescending parting comment, but at present, I'd forgive him almost anything. Hell, after the news he'd given me, Dr. Nicaragua was starting to look even more handsome. I combed my hair with my fingers out of habit, realizing as my fingers made contact that there was only half a head of hair to run through, but I guessed it would grow back.

As he left the room, I straightened my items and stash of paper on the hospital table with precision. I was just pushing the nib of the pen onto the paper when the door opened a crack.

"Ms. Shields? Ms. Gypsy Shields?"

Who the hell was this now? Was it some new character to find as many unique and interesting ways as possible to prod and evaluate me? I pulled up the covers, hoping to look a bit more respectable if such a thing was possible. I decided to give whoever it was the benefit of a slight nod as I sat a little bit straighter, adjusting the pillows behind me to complete the look.

"My name is Detective Constable Reardon from the Carlton police station. I'm hoping you remember me from our dinner last Saturday. My name's Connor." He ventured into the room until I saw all of him. He was taller than I remembered, and of course, much more handsome.

My heart leapt in my chest and I laughed, fanning myself with a magazine. Nay had come through for me. She'd actually gone to the police station and asked for Connor and now, here he was right in front of me. Then the second realization struck. In front of me was Connor from Saturday night, seeing me with a half-shaved head and staples across my scalp.

"Ergh. Yes," I said intelligently, my hand going up in a self-conscious gesture before I waved at him in a wild greeting.

"A police report has been filed. I'm hoping for more information. Your niece, Renee, told me about your injury and gave the impression you were having trouble talking. Can you tell me about what you saw on Saturday night by writing it down?" Seated beside me, Connor pulled out a writing pad to take notes. His head tilted to one side as his pen hovered over the paper. His smile seemed to build as it slowly lit up his face.

I grabbed the pen with my right hand and shuffled the paper across my table trolley. It was going to be a whole lot easier to write than speak in this scenario. With Connor only inches away, I didn't trust myself to speak, even if I could.

I wrote in my now shaky old lady script:

Walking home after dinner Saturday night, I saw man in an alleyway attack a girl-hit in head-drags girl away. Connor looked across at me, tipping his head before closing his eyes. I guessed the trembling muscle in his cheek signaled the moment when he fully grasped what had happened to me and he opened his eyes.

"Is this what happened after you left the restaurant Saturday night?" his tone was grave, voice low.

I was surprised. After twelve years in the force, surely he wasn't shocked by something like this? Perhaps he was struck by the nearness of it all. I suppose most of the witnesses or victims are strangers, and while we certainly weren't the best of friends yet, we did have a prior social connection, a very social connection I hoped. I had spoken to

Connor less than an hour before the young woman was abducted, possibly murdered.

"Can you go through what happened, Gypsy? Did you see the person that did this?"

I nodded and closed my eyes, shoulders shaking.

"Yes," I said, finding my voice a little bit more, pushing the pictures of violence out of my mind. "Horrible. He smelled funny, like acid, metallic." That was about all I could manage. Unable to speak clearly, I was awash with a mixture of emotions. I felt relieved that I was found and alive, confused and dazed that this was really happening, and frustrated that my body wouldn't do what I wanted it to. Most of all, the guilt tugged at my chest. Guilt that I was alive and the woman had met a fate yet to be determined.

I dug the heel of my palm into my chest, foraging around the bed for more tissues. I should be out there fighting for justice, striding by Connor's side to stalk the abductor, not passively waiting for my damn, disobedient body to heal. The disconnection between my mind and mouth wasn't helping.

Whilst in the past, I'd had foot-in-mouth disease, the opposite was worse; knowing exactly what I needed to say, but getting my mouth to cooperate and spit it out was taking a herculean effort.

"What happened, Gypsy?"

I scribbled with renewed intensity: *Will try my best to write. Computer would be easier. Can you get laptop?*

Connor looked at me, and I gestured for him to move around to my right. Carrying his chair effortlessly, he strode over to that side of my bed. Despite his confident steps, he didn't face me, his profile pale under his tan.

I scribbled the words with considerable effort. Although my progress was sluggish, the words came slowly but surely.

I was taken back to the fateful night at Sophia's. The memory came forward of leaving the restaurant, coming across the abduction in the alleyway, sensing the terror of the woman thrown into the van, making a frantic call to police, looking at the bottom of the vehicle. Then I focused on nothing but the details of the small identifying plate.

ZYB, that was it. ZYB, the first three letters of the registration plate. I scribbled them rapidly, tongue protruding in concentration. A dark, older style vehicle, pretty wide, maybe a Bedford van—surely, that should narrow things down. I thought about the voice and the build of the man. I remembered banging on the driver's window, then standing in front of the car, almost like a sitting duck, before he accelerated and the impact came, my head bouncing off the brick wall before I landed on the ground face-first.

There was something else, though. Coming back to the present, disengaging from my memories, I turned on my telepathic radar and tried initiating a connection with Connor, but I couldn't get a read. I desperately needed the information he had. He was holding back. I lowered my head to study him. I knew as soon as I revealed the registration plate details that Connor had retreated. A part of his mind was hidden, curled up and tucked away in the dark recesses that he wasn't sharing with anyone, especially me. Why would Connor keep this knowledge hidden? What was he trying to hide?

I would do my best to get it out of him. Secrets

were no way to begin if things were ever to go anywhere between us. However, Connor's face was a mask, solid and impervious.

He leaned back to look out the window, with his eyes unmoving and licking his lips.

"Well," said Connor, fiddling with a pen, "thank you, that's more information than I thought I'd get. I'll amend the report and update my colleagues."

"Tell me," I said, facing him with my chin held high.

"There's nothing to tell, Gypsy." He shuffled his feet slightly. Looking away quickly cementing his decision to keep his secrets to himself. He stood up, "The information will help, that much I know. I'll run it through the database and it will absolutely narrow things down."

I wasn't convinced. I'd been following the news of the kidnapping in the media and knew there was more to the investigation than this.

"We don't have much to go on at the moment. We have no CCTV footage, and information hasn't led anywhere positive at this stage. The pressure is on, so this will really make a difference. Thank you, Gypsy, for sending Renee to find me."

He grimaced and then blushed. How I wished this hadn't happened and we could be carefree and flirtatious, laughing and joking at a café somewhere.

I pursed my lips and cleared my throat. I'd known what I witnessed would be important, but hadn't realized the cops had so little to go on.

"Find him." Although I could only spit out a few words, my limited vocabulary could only mean hope. With a bit of luck and a whole lot of work with rehabilitation specialists, I would recover my ability to speak fluently.

"I'll leave my card. Ask someone to call if you need me. Otherwise, I'll be back soon with photographs and more info. Oh, yes, and a laptop." He handed the card over, aiming it at my left hand, and then paused briefly before flushing at the realization that I couldn't move it. I extended my right hand to him and smiled.

"Thanks. It's okay," I managed to say.

He nodded. "Actually, I can come back in a minute with a laptop. I can lend you my personal one for a couple of days. I think you need it more than I do." His mouth turned up slightly. At that moment, I wondered if there was an understanding, a mutual attraction, but damn it, I'd made that mistake before. I was far too old to make a fool of myself again, although who the hell was I to worry about foolishness? I had a shaved, stapled head and controlling my own saliva had proved a distinct challenge.

"I'll be back." He stepped over to the door, where he paused to look at me before leaving.

What was he not telling me, and why not?

The hour grew late and I knew it was time to go to sleep, but I struggled with insomnia, so it might not happen for hours yet. My questions remained unanswered. Did Connor feel the attraction that I did? Would he find the killer? Was the young woman still alive? What was Connor hiding from me, and why?

I wrestled with sleep for what felt like an eternity before it finally claimed me.

*****

5

Renee sat on the edge of the chair, inhaling the smell of whiteboard markers and exercise books. She loved the stillness and quiet before the bell rang. She opened the drawer, and there was the locket. She froze, swallowing hard, feeling heat in her ears and cheeks. *That damn David had put it back.* She'd left it under his desk earlier that morning, thinking she'd solved the problem. Looking around to confirm no one else was there, she shuffled her feet. As the door opened behind her, she realized her classmates were starting to trickle in. She moved her head to within inches of the desktop, strands of hair falling forward. Renee wrinkled her forehead, doodling on the paper in the middle of her desk.

They were assigned tables of eight, and over the last few months, she had gotten to know a few of her companions. As the students sat down, she could feel David's eyes on her, burning holes in her skin. She put a wall of energy up, wishing him out of existence.

Mr. Ganner strode in, arms swinging, as the bell rang. His voice boomed through the room.

"Well, good morning, class of 7G," he rumbled, a smile slicing his long, lined face. He was strict, but Renee remembered his kindness, how he'd helped her after class with quiet talks, listening to her awkward description of life since Dad had moved out, his brown eyes registering her awkwardness and pain, unable to put any of it into words.

"Now let's start with homework. Who wrote their essay? I'm sure you did, Janie." The classroom went from silence to an irritating scrape of drawers as they tugged out their exercise books.

"What's wrong with you, David?" Jenny rolled her eyes with a hard smile.

Renee couldn't help herself. "He's upset because I saw the locket he left hidden in my desk. The one he stole from his sister. The one I don't want anymore." She scowled until her jaw hurt, the beginnings of a headache with a tight band across her forehead.

Mr. Ganner was speaking again. "Right, that's enough. You can sort that out later. For now, let's start with Gareth. Would you like to read your essay out to the class?"

Gareth began his hesitant and robotic reading aloud and Renee focused quietly on her own essay, shutting David out of existence. She suffered through the remaining hour and a half until the recess bell rang. Renee joined the mass of students shoving their books away before racing towards the bottleneck of the door. As she shuffled her way through the throng of children to the playground, the chill air washed over her. She pushed out a breath, watching warm white circles rise in the icy air.

Renee stood with one foot propped against the wall. Jenny strode over and stood directly in front of her.

"What was that about with David?" Her round eyes scanned Renee's face. Her brown hair was so silky it hung in perfect sheets. Renee remembered a recent jealous look at Jenny's beautiful hair. Renee admired Jenny's looks even if she annoyed her at times.

"Oh, he walked me home from school one day. I was never sure about him. He asked me over to his place last week, and his Mum and sister weren't home. It was a bit weird. Then he gave me some jewelry, which didn't feel right, especially after I found out he stole it from his sister's room. He's been nasty to me ever since," she said, picking at her nails.

"Oh…" said Jenny. Her mouth was pinched so tightly, she seemed to be in pain. Renee was getting a bit tired of Jenny, the social inquisitor, interfering in friendships, trying to fix things. "Why don't I go and talk to him for you?"

"No!" Foot bouncing Renee fiddled with her necklace. "*Don't* go and talk to him. I'll just ignore him and he'll leave me alone."

Jenny had already left. Why did she have to keep sticking her nose in?

She rubbed her arms feeling the cold, and looked around the playground. Her gaze darted to various groups around the yard before deciding on a couple of friends who were talking in the corner, thinking she might invite them to walk around a bit. Here was Jenny, back already, out of breath and eyes shining, obviously keen to pass on some juicy morsel.

"I talked to him. He says he's upset that you're going out with someone else."

Renee shook her head. "Well, that's funny. I don't remember going out with anyone else, but obviously, *he* does. If he believes that kind of thing…well…that suits me just fine, because he's a weirdo anyway."

"What do you mean, he's a weirdo?"

"Would you invite a boy back to your place when you knew your Mum and Dad weren't home? And then go through your sister's room and find something to steal to give to your new boyfriend?" Renee wrinkled her nose. She didn't want to be his girlfriend, anyway. He was giving her the creeps. Jenny's tale explained why he'd been picking on her lately though.

"I guess not." Jenny chewed on her lip. She slowly drifted into one of the many knots of children scattered across the playground.

Renee spent the rest of the day pretending she couldn't feel David's looks, which alternated between scowls and curious adoration. She was glad of the distraction of geography, mainly maps and rain followed by spelling and corrections to take her through to the end of the day.

She said a silent thank you as the final bell rang and she queued up at the classroom door.

Today she was glad that home wasn't far. She slotted on her backpack and pushed through the exit. She quickened her footsteps. David used a similar route, and she didn't want him to come running to catch up.

She wondered why bad things kept happening, one after the other. First Dad had moved out, and then Gypsy was attacked. Now David had started picking on her because of his stupid personality. Her instinct told her that he could be needy and desperate, even if she hadn't fully articulated it—it was simply a cloud of knowing.

Her shoulders tightened as a car slowed behind her. Turning her head, she saw a young guy leering at her through the window of his black van, his blond head a mass of curls and his face was dirty. The car slowed down again and heart pounding even further, Renee shoved her hands under her armpits.

"Hello, gorgeous." His smile was hard and dangerous, his eyes cold.

She felt her leg muscles tightening, ready to run.

"Don't be scared, your aunt sent me, you know Gypsy? Get in." The car had almost stopped, and over its purring engine, his voice was low and rumbling, sending a race of prickles up her back.

"Go away! I'll scream…" Her voice sounded shrill and distant.

"Aw, come on, don't be like that." His snort became uncontrolled laughter. Hitching her bag higher, she ran with no destination in mind, her breath ragged, as she sped past houses.

She heard him calling in the distance, "Tell Gypsy I said hi, okay?" Then the engine revved as he overtook her, blaring the horn in a long loud blast. She stopped on the corner, gasping for air, legs wobbly. As the thump in her chest slowed from a pounding to a soft beat, she realized she was just a few houses away from home. Renee sagged against the wall, whispering a thank you. Her thoughts were jumbled, and she walked quickly, counting the seconds before she got home.

She arrived home out of breath, and took a turn into the driveway. Renee stopped to compose herself. Then she unlocked the front door and dumped her school bag on the floor. She threw herself into the closest chair, staring at the wall. The house was hushed and she wished desperately for Leah to get home from work early.

She closed her eyes and fell into an armchair, head

down. After a few seconds, she clomped upstairs to her room and threw herself onto the bed with a whimper. The familiar feel of her bed comforted her as she wrapped the covers around her body, the cocoon offering safety and security. She'd escaped and her terror had subsided.

She heard the downstairs door bang closed.

Throwing off the covering, she sat bolt upright, ran out to the landing, and jumped down the stairs, taking them two at a time.

"Mum? *Mum*!"

She sprinted for the kitchen.

Empty table, empty chairs, and no signs of life.

"Hello? Mum?"

She rushed to the dining room, searching in a wide arc.

There was her mother, her body sagging in the chair.

"Mum? Mum? *Mum*!"

"What? Oh, sorry, Renee. Yes, I'm here."

"Something's happened."

Leah's head jerked up. "What do you mean, something's happened?"

"A man followed me home from school, told me to get in the car, and he said he knew Gypsy."

"What? When, just now? Oh, my God." Leah was up in one swift motion, reaching for her daughter.

"I'm all right. It just scared me a bit, that's all." She reached out to Leah for comfort, and let out a quiet moan, grasping her mother's waist. She wanted to tell her everything, but wasn't sure where to start.

"I was shaking, but I'm all right now. I love you, Mum. I'm so glad to be home." Her speech was muffled by Leah's spontaneous squeeze, and they stood swaying for a moment. "Jesus, I can't believe this. Wait until I talk to Gypsy. We're going to have to report this."

"Sounds good," Leah agreed.

Renee buried her face into her mother's chest, enjoying the comfort while it lasted.

Renee would check on Gyp and tell her about what happened. Gyp owed her big time, at least two movie visits and a long session of shopping. Once her aunt was better, she'd be making sure all benefits were paid in full.

*****

After leaving the laptop on her bedside table, Connor snuck out from the room, leaving a snoring Gypsy behind. He'd found a packet of six piles of post-it notes in the car and left them on her table. What a god-awful shock that was when he saw her after surgery. Of course, he'd visited victims in hospitals before, but this was different. He felt the nausea take hold, muscles cramping and his temperature rising. He wanted to hold her and promise that he could make it all go away and that he wouldn't let anyone else hurt her. This was different from the one-night stands. He knew they could be friends, if given the time. He wanted to know her. Gypsy listened when he talked, and looked at him in a way that he thought revealed interest. The split with Jill had brought some finality to what he knew was a performance, an exercise in routine. They had been actors in a play with the roles set years ago, true intimacy was a thing of the past.

If what he suspected was true, his life and career

was about to change, his love life for the better, and his career down the toilet. He sighed, hoping he was simply being overly dramatic.

After the shock of seeing Gypsy injured, Connor had begun to wonder about the man that knocked her over. His build, the timbre of his voice, the van, and the registration details of the vehicle seemed to be pointing in one direction. A direction he didn't want to think about. He muttered to himself as he headed for the car, hands clenching into fists.

"Won't let it happen," mumbled Connor.

Scenes from years past came back to him. Pets were found at home killed and left in a gruesome display, questions about serious incidents at school, and the assault on his niece, Christie, which she had been so damn tight lipped about.

It couldn't be, though; there were some things he knew Aaron wasn't capable of. Connor would confirm it soon enough. He was driving now, heading toward Clifton Hill, where cafes and bars spilled out onto the street with tables, chairs, and umbrellas jostling for position. Hipsters and hippies wearing the latest green hair, rainbow berets, or designer shoes were the common denominator here. Most of them were deep in conversation but still aware of seeing and being seen, flicking glances over their shoulders at regular intervals.

Jaw set, he focused on driving, his movements precise. He turned into a side street, and then pulled into a narrow lane before his tiny home. Scraping his car through this street was a nightmare, particularly as built-in garages were few and far between, and parking spaces rare.

The usual musty smell greeted him as he opened

the front door. When he'd split with Jill, his mind was not fully on the task of finding somewhere to live. He'd viewed this empty unit, its unloved air with orange worn carpet and grey kitchen benches barely registering. He'd taken it and moved in his sparse belongings with little time or attention on making it a home.

He threw his keys and briefcase on the dining table, heading to the kitchen to see if there was anything in the refrigerator worth eating. His brows pulled down at the contents: shriveled carrots, a six-pack of beer that he'd bought months before, dried up cheese, curled ham, and a couple of yogurts. He chose yogurt, spooning it into his mouth mechanically.

He looked out through the inky kitchen windows. All was dark and quiet in the endless blackness of the late hour.

Connor remembered that he should check his gun, and his head snapped up. Connor raced to his bedroom and knelt, barely registering the covers in disarray, the pillow on the floor, or the sheet peeling off the mattress as he foraged underneath. He dragged the box out, horrified that the lock had been broken and was hanging lopsided. Yet, the gun was in the box. He let out a breath and sagged against the bed. He stared at his palms. *Who would have broken the lock and left the gun behind?*

Did he leave it unlocked like that? That wasn't like him, but there'd been a lot on his mind since Aaron stopped replying to his messages and calls.

If anyone knew where Aaron was, Tiran would. Pushing himself up, Connor reached for the phone in his back pocket and dialed.

"Tiran?"

"Connor? What's going on?"

"I'm sorry to call so late, but I'm looking for Aaron. Is he there?"

"No."

Picking at flaky bits of paint on a picture, he waited for her to go on.

"I don't know where he is." Her monotone registered loud and clear, jarring him out of his distracted state. "We had a bust up Saturday and I haven't seen him since. Hopefully he's at a mate's place and won't be back 'til he's cooled down. Probably not for a while if my black eye is anything to go by. I need time to calm down myself."

"A black eye? I'll be right over."

"Hang on, Connor." He hung up, collected his keys, and rushing out the door, he ran for the car to head to Tiran and Aaron's place.

On the way, thoughts rolled through his mind and he felt the sweat forming on his upper lip. He focused on his hands gripping the steering wheel. Could he have prevented this? Somehow, he had failed his nephew. He'd done everything he could to support him, or thought he had, but unlike his sister, Christie, Aaron had never really moved on from his father's death and his mother's plunge into alcoholism. If only Aaron had come to Connor. Aaron had gone through a phase where he dabbled in drugs for a few months, but he thought he'd moved past that.

Pulling into the driveway of the beige, cement sheet house, Connor saw that Tiran had left the porch light on for him. She was opening the front door as he stopped the car at the end of the driveway. He shifted in his seat as he saw the door open, the light shining across the porch steps.

"Tiran."

"Connor, come in. It's a bit of a mess." She gestured with a dismissive sweep of the arm. The lounge room was large enough, furnished with a brown velvet couch and plastic toys strewn across the grey carpet, and bright multi-colored baby rug with mirrors and plastic rings sewn in. Their home looked lived in, but nothing shocking, considering there was a ten month old in the house.

"What's going on? You've got a black eye?" He felt a thickness in his throat.

"Yeah." Connor could see the side of her face, purple and swollen in the shadows. Tiran was holding her face at a strange angle and she touched its tender contours. "This was a one off. You know that, right? He's not like that. Well, not usually anyway. This is the first time." She sank into the chair opposite him. She was less animated than usual and he watched her sagging form in the chair, barely moving.

"I know that, Tiran. He's a good guy, just a lot going on with work and a new baby. It can take a while to find your way."

"He hasn't been himself. I don't know…maybe more paranoid than usual. He asked me who the other bloke was, as if I have time with a ten month old baby!" Tiran stood up, ran her hands through her hair, and then pulled the belt in her dirty white dressing gown tighter.

She looked at Connor, the skin around her eyes pinched with sleep deprivation. Connor realized how lucky his nephew was. He had a woman who loved him, supported him, and did a great job caring for their baby boy.

"Bailey asleep?" asked Connor, standing up. "Mind if I look in on him?"

"Yeah, c-come through," she stuttered, rubbing the back of her neck. They padded through to the boy's bedroom, where a child's lamp cast a dim light across the cot. The word "Bailey" was spelled out in blue letters across the wall along with pictures of Tigger and Winnie the Pooh. The cot and drawers were of a freshly varnished dark timber with a matching changing table. Connor and Tiran gazed into the cot and there he was, blond, soft, and beautiful, cherub-like in sleep. Connor tenderly ran his hand over the boy's head, letting out his breath slowly, and then let the back of his fingers rest against Bailey's velvety cheek.

"Thank you," he said quietly before pulling away. He paused on the threshold of the room. "Tell me that mark on your face isn't from a fist."

She finally pulled her gaze away from her son to leave the room after Connor, who made way for her to pass.

"I reckon we could do with a coffee." Her voice was a monotone, her steps shuffling as she led him to the tiled kitchen, and Connor noticed her hair was greasy, unwashed. She flicked the yellow kettle switch and turned, hands hanging limply by her side. "What's got into him? Do you know, because I've been driving myself mad? I can't do it anymore."

Connor rolled his arms in their sockets, and then crossed them, watching this process as if his limbs belonged to someone else. Then he brought his head up to speak.

"He'd be more likely to tell you than me. I hoped after he stopped smoking joints last year that things were on the way up."

"Well, for a while they were." He could almost smell the hopelessness. She had given up. "He started carrying on about cops, how corrupt they were, they had it in for him, and that I might be sneaking around and seeing other blokes. I'm worn out. Bailey's teething. I'm doing all I can just to get through each day." She pulled the cups out of the cupboard, swinging them across to the bench with a bang. When she fetched a spoon, her belt got caught as she closed the cutlery drawer with a slam, and she jerked it out impatiently.

"I'm sorry, I don't see him as much as I used to." Connor rubbed the side of his nose and his forehead. "I didn't want to interfere. When he surfaces, will you ask him to call me? I've sent him texts and tried ringing him, but he's turned the phone off and gone to ground."

"I know. Maybe he's ashamed enough that he's put himself into exile. Sounds like it. I need some space myself. Maybe we can start again after this. After this, we need a fresh beginning. Wish we could get a break, just for a while."

He sipped on the hot coffee as he tried to find the right words. He wondered where the hell Aaron was. He wanted to ask her more questions, but realized it would only make everything worse for Tiran. Things hadn't been easy for Aaron when they took him in. First, the courthouse explosion, which killed his brother Dan, then his wife Rae fell apart, alcohol becoming her best friend. After the house fire, he and Jill had taken both Christie and Aaron in. Rae had fallen asleep smoking, yet again, with fatal consequences. Thankfully, the fire department got the kids out in time. Connor just assumed they'd all moved past that. It was a hell of a long time ago.

He paced restlessly, pausing to settle the cup on the bench and run his fingers through his hair. The family had suffered two funerals in twelve months, and although the tragedy had become less raw over the years, he wondered if it still got to Aaron. If he could get through to him, tell him things might be tough, but they'd work it out together, he could help him.

As he backed away, Connor shook his head, wondering if he was kidding himself, until he was ready to face the tornado that would catapult them into the next part of the nightmare.

*****

After punching in the code to the station's security door, Connor headed for his desk, glancing at the clock as he marched down the corridor of pale brown carpet tiles. Despite his run that morning, he felt strained to the limit, stress levels peaking. Halfway down the corridor, he paused and stared into the tinted window of the chief's office. No chief yet, thank God. At the end of the corridor, he reached the open squad room, which held six formations of four desks, most of them empty. He was hoping at this early hour that he'd catch Ian Robson, his partner for the last two years.

"Hey, Connor! You're here early—what happened, wet the bed again?" Ian smirked as he leaned all the way back in his office chair, a friendly jeer plastered across his face. Ian's hair was greying at the temples in stark contrast to the rest of his jet-black mop. The bottom of his shirt was already stained with tomato sauce and untucked to reveal the saggy bottom of his beer belly. He wore dark rectangular glasses, giving the false impression he had the potential for intellectual debate.

Unlike many of his counterparts, Connor ignored Ian's rude jibes. He knew Ian 'Robbo' Robson enjoyed a high case close rate, and accepted his eccentricities, even if his abrasiveness rubbed most of his colleagues the wrong way.

"Not this time. Might have a lead for the boys upstairs."

"Oh yeah, which case? Not the big mover and shaker, the missing headquarters spy admin girl who took off with the reports, Cinderella look alike?"

"How did you guess?" said Connor as he slid down in his chair, his voice strained.

"Maybe because it's all anyone can talk about. No damn leads other than wackos who saw someone look at them funny and they're damn sure the stranger is the perp. Why did she have to stir the shit by stealing bloody reports?"

"Well, I got something on that, might have a lead…" Connor chose his words carefully as he rubbed at his temple.

"Go on, then." With a squeak, Ian roused himself from his chair to perch on the corner of Connor's desk, fidgeting with the penholder. "What have you got? Surprise me."

"Well, maybe something. Possible witness in the hospital assaulted and left for dead."

"Oh yeah, but are they still breathing? Talking? Wish I'd known about it earlier. I haven't seen you for ages. Wouldn't be a chick now, would it?" Robbo's eyes were bloodshot and he scratched at a mark on his arm.

Connor paused, his fingers hanging over the keyboard, and glared at Ian. "Now listen, Robbo, you and me go back a long way. You know how I operate, and she isn't a chick, she's a woman." He swatted at a fly, which had already disappeared.

"Hooo well, *excuse* me! A wo-man! As opposed to the red headed chick and the blonde floozies you took home; the one-night stands I wasn't supposed to know about? Doesn't take you long, mate, must be rough being a chick magnet."

Shit, how did he know? Connor thought he'd been discreet.

"Give it a rest, Robbo. This is important." He glanced at his phone as if it might somehow ring, rocking back and forth on his swivel chair.

"'Course it is, dickhead, or you and me wouldn't be here. All I'm asking for is details. If you don't give them to me now, maybe I'll try elsewhere."

"Don't start, Ian, not now. I *mean* it!" Connor turned away and was up and out of his chair in an instant, beating a path to the tearoom.

"Hey, hey, hey, don't get all hot under the collar." Ian was trailing behind, the scent of a lead luring him down the corridor. The office was starting to wake up. Phones had started ringing, and curious heads had popped up from cubicles. The light was on in the chief's office, but still no chief. "We both know how the politics goes with the powers that be. I guess what I'm saying is, spill your guts. It's not like you to be coy, big boy. What's going on?" Ian's smile didn't reflect in his narrowed eyes.

Connor grabbed a mug from the rack and started spooning in coffee and sugar. He sighed as the hot water cascaded into the chipped mug. "Her name's

Gypsy. I met her at a dinner Saturday night. Nice lady. Then Monday, a little girl comes into the station asking for me, telling me her aunt's been hurt, witness to a kidnapping. I visit the hospital, and there she is— head shaved, post-surgery, can't talk. One side of her body is paralyzed, pretty damn serious."

"No shit, Sherlock."

"You always had a way with words." As he stirred the cup, Connor walked slowly back to his desk, Ian trailing beside him slightly. "So last night, I went to see her at St. Vincent's. She can't talk, but she can write. She told me what happened. She didn't get a look at the guys face, but she saw him take the girl and load her into a wide, dark van, maybe a Bedford."

"Don't suppose she saw the plates in the dark?"

"Well, you supposed wrong…"

"She did! Well, now we're talking. Thank God for that! We might get those monkeys off our fucking back for at least five minutes while they get ready for the next press gig." Ian's posture was slumped.

"First things first, Ian. I need to amend the Grievous Bodily Harm charge report. Then we can chase down this partial plate."

"Well, what's the partial? I can run a search to narrow it down and start paying some visits."

"Okay, Robbo, but stay with me on this. This one's personal." Connor opened a desk drawer before foraging for his antacids.

"They all are, mate."

"No, this one might be more personal than I want." Connor drew in his shoulders.

"What the hell are you talking about?"

"A hunch, an instinct, but I hope I'm wrong. Maybe after we pay a visit to the van driver, we could take a trip down memory lane. Humor me, okay?"

"What do you mean, you'd like to be wrong? You started playing with your imaginary friends again? I've been humoring you for years, Connor." Robbo turned quickly, startled by one of the administration staff hurling a bunch of papers into the security bin.

"Funny guy." The click of the keys was getting louder and Connor clenched his teeth. "Up to you. You can come, or you can stay here with your feet up. Either way, I'm pretty sure this is a break the family's been searching for." *Although, not the break that Christie has been hoping for, or Jill.*

"Right, here we go. Bedford vans with ZYB in Victoria—if it is a Bedford van."

"Well, there's only two showing up. One is nearby in Brunswick, the other out in Laverton, looks like it belongs to a factory or warehouse," said Robbo looking across at Connor.

"Who's the one in Brunswick?"

"Stewart Johnson. I'll look him up and see what he's been up to."

"What about the one in Laverton?"

"Jeremy O'Connell."

"I thought so. That hunch…" Connor blinked rapidly, feeling his face go slack.

"Connor, I swear to God…don't go all strong and silent on me, you're not the type. Who's this Jeremy O'Connell, your long lost fucking cousin? Remember when I told you not to hold out on me." Ian was pacing now, stomping back and forth in front of their desks and waving his hands.

"In or out? You've got thirty seconds." Connor grabbed his jacket and keys and the sprint down the corridor was on.

"Seriously, Connor, what the hell is going on?" Robbo's voice wavered as he walked faster, his bulky frame struggling to keep up.

"By the end of the day, we'll know."

*****

6

It had been a tortuous day, but a productive one. When I woke up, I found a pack of Post-it sticky notes on the table, wondering if they were left by Connor. I rolled my eyes and with a snort, wondered when I'd get over my bias for yellow ones. I could think of more romantic gifts, but it did mean he was thinking of me, considerate man that he was. I unwrapped them with one hand, snatched the pink, blue and green ones and tossed them in the bin, holding on to the important yellow ones which I left on the table. Later in the morning, I'd met Lyndall the torture specialist, otherwise known as the rehabilitation girlie. She'd introduced herself in her over-the-top cheery way and talked me into a wheelchair. I hated the idea of a wheelchair. They were always something I associated with invalids or the elderly, and I didn't want to be labelled as either. Lyndall had tiptoed in while I was drinking tea and eating biscuits, catching me off guard, a stream of crumbs decorated my pajamas. Earlier, I had started reading a book and I'd dropped it as I dozed off. I awoke, and sat bolt upright as the Channel 7 news came on. I felt the vibration in my throat, a high-pitched squeal.

Holy shit!

This was her. I knew it, felt it. Joanne Seyers, employee of Victoria Police—of all the bloody irony, a police administrator—had disappeared Saturday night after an evening out in Carlton. There were no leads and police had scoured closed circuit television footage with what looked like no joy. As her picture flashed again, the same one I'd seen in the paper, I realized how beautiful she was, so blonde, with gorgeous porcelain skin accentuating her youth.

I felt the tears gather, my body sagging against the pillow. I covered my mouth with my right hand, my attention riveted on the screen.

Her gorgeous brother—who shared a flat with her, he'd sent her an SMS with no reply. Then he sent another an hour later, and an hour later. What the hell was that like? What did he go through? When she didn't come home by morning, he'd gone to the police. My heart hurt for him. After three days now, he'd expect the worst.

We'll get him, I promise you, we'll all get him, Connor, Renee, and me. When we do, he'll pay.

So when Lyndall arrived later to usher me off to rehabilitation, I tried bargaining with her, making excuses. I wanted to go home but she wasn't having it. Muttering curses under my breath, I felt my stomach harden.

"Not now, I can't. I need to use the phone, find out what's happening, I'm the only witness."

"I understand that, but while you're in the hospital, it's vital you focus on getting well, not distract yourself. Off we go, I'll bring the chair around so you can ease yourself into it slowly." She was bright and cheery, but as she pushed up her sleeves and breezed her way to my bedside, I realized arguing with her would be a waste of time.

I levered myself into the chair and she quickly wheeled me down the corridor. I tapped my fingers on the arm of the wheelchair. I needed to play an active part in the investigation, not sit here doing nothing. I'd never been good at waiting.

Lyndall took me into a huge room filled with gymnastic mats, large fitness balls and the most noticeable instrument of torture, the walking bars. I blanched, bringing a shaky hand to my forehead, feeling my chest caving in as I let out a whimper.

As I pushed myself up out of the chair, Lyndall helped. She kneeled at one end of the bars, which looked like something fit for an Olympic gymnast, and chanted supposedly soothing words such as, "That's it, keep going. It will get easier each day, I promise." She watched on, squatting at the end of the bars, as I willed my limbs seemingly attached to marionette like strings, to move across pitifully. In some twisted madness, I wished the left side of my body was still numb. At least that way, it wouldn't hurt like *hell*. As I sagged back into the wheelchair at the end of my crawl, gasping for breath, my eardrums felt ready to burst from the ringing in my ears.

"Well done," praised Lyndall, but I couldn't speak. We headed back to the room. A dark haired nurse leaned over the counter as we reached her.

"A visitor left this for you earlier." She handed a card to me.

A visitor left me a note?

I looked down at a smooth cream envelope with the word "Gypsy" typed across the front.

Inside was a green Post-it note. I shuddered, a shiver going down my back. The note read simply:

Your niece is cute. Keep your mouth shut.

I lifted my shoulders slightly, rocking my upper body and closing my eyes as the chair reached the side of my bed.

He'd found me.

I dragged a palm down my right leg and let out a quiet moan.

"You okay?" said Lyndall.

I couldn't answer. Renee, my beautiful blonde girl, was in danger. He'd tracked us down, although how in the hell he did it, I had no idea.

As Lyndall helped me back into bed, my attention remained fixed on the note. I managed to lift my head to deliver a forced grin.

Lyndall left with a tight smile of her own and I leaned back against the bed. Leah whirled into the room, her face red. She planted her feet squarely at the bottom of my bed and pointed at me.

"I don't care how sick you are, I want some answers, *now*. Start talking."

Icy cold silence. I wondered where Renee was.

"He found me," I said my voice flat and expressionless.

"He found Renee and almost took her!" She pointed at me, her arm straight, eyes bulging, her breathing raspy. Renee was cowering behind her, unable to look at either of us.

I looked down at my trembling hands. I couldn't meet Leah's eyes. I suppressed the desire to run from the room, helped by the fact that my bloody legs wouldn't cooperate anyway.

I heard the newsreader's voice coming from the

TV. Talk about rotten timing, the media was squeezing every drop out of the excruciating story. Joanne Seyers beautiful face was plastered across the screen, the newsreader's high-pitched voice terrifying us with the tragic tale of a beautiful blonde and her inconsolable brother. I snatched the remote to switch it off.

"Leave it," snarled Leah through gritted teeth. "So what do I do now, huh? Now that he knows where her school is, how do I stop him from getting to her? Do I have to keep her home? She should have known better. I'll have to report this, the *last* thing we need right now …"

"Leave her. Not her fault."

"I know it's not, for God's sake. Don't tell me how to speak to my own daughter! I'm so over your holier than thou attitude. It's *not* her fault, but you damn well have made it her problem now. What the hell were you thinking?"

Oh God, here we go. I made sure the laptop Connor had left was powered up. I would need it as part of the inferno that had been lit. I poised my shaking fingers over the keyboard.

"What did Gypsy drag you into?" Leah peered at her daughter, her face crimson.

"She didn't drag me into anything," said Renee quietly, looking at the floor. Yet, her red face gave her away. Poor girl—how the hell she put up with Leah as a mother for all these years was beyond me.

I wished I could bloody well speak, but at that moment, bashing the keyboard would have to do. I was in the hospital with a brain bleed, for God's sake; didn't that mean I got a break here? Offer me some sort of protection from my crazy enraged sister?

The night I left the restaurant, I interrupted an attack. It was that woman on TV. I remembered the license plate and van. I didn't see the bastard's face but heard his voice. I was on the phone to police when he knocked me over. I needed help to report it, could not speak. I typed as best I could and roughly turned the laptop around to show Leah the screen. Her face seemed almost purple, her fists clenched and teeth gritted.

"So why the hell did you make her part of this? Why was it so *vital* to put her in danger? You could have written it down for someone else! This better be *damn* good, I swear." If her color didn't subside soon, they'd set up a bed for her in the next room right after she popped a major blood vessel.

I typed like mad on the laptop, slamming each key. There was no way in hell I'd be able to spit out the onslaught of emotions raging through me.

We lifted our heads as the door creaked open. Nurse Tina stuck her head in. "Everything all right?"

Her tone wasn't aggressive, but she'd obviously heard the yelling.

Leah bit her lip, staring at me before sitting down and glaring at Tina, her expression sullen. "Its fine, we're just a bit emotional right now. The man that abducted that woman could have killed Gypsy, and he followed her niece home today, my daughter. We're still in the thick of it all." Leah frowned at Tina, opposing her.

"Yes, I understand, I really do, but that sounds like a police matter. It's a fraught situation and of course, emotions are high. Brain injury patients are monitored carefully, especially the first few days afterwards. Your sister's making good progress and we don't want to risk any set-backs, so we're trying to keep stimulation down to a minimum." Tina's lips pressed together firmly, and she glared at both of us.

The door closed firmly.

"Jesus, this place is a freaking circus!" hissed Leah, who had edged so far out from the seat that I wondered if she would fall off.

"Mum, can I go get a drink?" Renee ducked her head, her voice quiet. I didn't blame her for wanting to get the hell out of there. The tension was giving me a headache and I hadn't had one of those since, well since some random stranger ran me over and left me for dead.

"You haven't ever grown up, have you? Is that why you and Renee are friends? Two kids who understand each other?" Leah frowned and pushed out a sharp flow of air, reaching down into her purse. She grabbed a five-dollar bill and shoved it at Renee. Renee didn't want to come out from behind her wall of hair. Instead, she slunk off to hide in the hospital canteen down in the bowels of the building somewhere.

What the hell? Don't be ridiculous, Leah, we both know how old I am...

"You know exactly what I'm talking about. For once in your life be *honest* with yourself!" Standing up, she moved closer to the bed, pointing at me. Traces of sweat had appeared on her forehead.

I looked at the doorway, feeling dizzy, my chest tightening. Finally, this was it. This was the watershed moment I had been searching for so many years ago, a chance to clear the air, get the ugliness out in the open, and maybe restore our previous closeness. Yet, if she wanted it to happen at that very moment, I wasn't prepared. Surely, she could have waited until I was feeling a bit stronger, when life had resumed its routine, the mouse wheel spinning relentlessly. Not now, not like this.

Had to get her to police. Met cop. Connor. She sent him here.

"Where the hell was I? You involved a minor in reporting a crime? Jesus, Gypsy, what is *wrong* with you? When were you two going to give up this stupid little game of secrets? Oh, that's right, dumb Leah, dumb as dog shit."

Leah's anger seemed to have peaked. She turned away from me, covering her face with her hands before spinning back.

"The little messages you think I can't see, answering each other's questions when not one of you talked. I'm not smart enough to know about any of it, am I? Please, spare me." She folded her arms and glared at me.

"Jealous," I managed to grunt, "You jealous?"

"Jealous? She's my daughter, not yours, always has been, always will be. I'm her mother, not her best friend. I know you two are close. Maybe you should go find a man and have your own kids, Gypsy. Maybe that way you'll have something to worry about."

"*Bitch*! You. Bitch!" was all that I could manage. The sweat settled across my forehead, my breathing heavy so that I struggled to slow it down.

My spine straightened, fingernails biting into my palms. My head was thumping harder and I wished she'd leave. The nurse was right. This was not the time or the place for family therapy. I wondered if it really was better to have this out in the open or to let it be. Did it need to be sorted out at this very moment?

"You think it was easy for me, Gypsy? Staying home while you were out, listening to Dad defend you when I was at home? It was obvious to all of us who he loved best, and when I asked him, he wouldn't answer. How do you think that felt?"

"Almost twenty years later…"

"Yeah, maybe it is twenty years later, but some scars never heal. You took to the bottle and ran yourself into the ground, not caring about anyone else. Did you not think about what that did to us? But he could never see it, not with you, the smart beautiful one that looked just like him."

"My fault?" Heat formed in my gut.

"Whose is it, then?"

I remembered one of the most hellish phases of my young life, my late teens, early twenties. I went through my angry young woman stage. I hated life, men and everything they represented. Tired of the screaming slinging matches between Mum and Dad, night after night, before finally they separated, I turned to alcohol in a big way. All the while, I told myself it was just a phase, but it was a damn long phase. It lasted nearly eighteen months. Eventually, I realized I was on a slippery slope and one day I'd wind up dead or a vegetable from too many close calls.

Thankfully, I'd had the sense to check myself into rehab and never went back to the bottle. As much as I wanted to strangle my sister, she had a point. Wrapped up in my own pain, I hadn't thought about what it did to my family. I used my ability to get in touch with Renee when I could, but never to contact Leah. I hadn't been interested in her world, even though she was my *sister*, for God's sake.

"Maybe a bit selfish sometimes," I managed to say, squeezing out the words. Even if they were begrudging, they were out, hanging in the air. My chin hit my chest.

"What?" she said quietly. She lifted her head.

I'd never bothered getting to know Leah, her thoughts, her pictures, how things felt from her viewpoint. I'd let resentment pool like a caustic poison seeping through my pores.

I beckoned her over to the bed. She scowled at me before her glare moved off to the window, then the ceiling, the headboard. She shuffled over and sat on the bed. I held out my hand, and when she snuck hers out from her lap, I grabbed hold of it tightly.

For the first time I could remember, I made the effort and dug for pictures. They came thick and fast. I saw Leah standing at the kitchen window of our old home, staring out into the backyard. My sixteenth birthday party—that disco was a riot—Leah got a night out at the local thirty-seat bistro. There was twelve-year-old Leah sitting bolt upright in bed in the early hours of the morning, her skin prickling. After shifting her head from side to side birdlike, she padded over to my bed and crouched over, discovering I wasn't there. I saw her take a sharp intake of breath, putting one hand over her mouth, and then crawl back into bed and pull the covers over her head, sniffing quietly. Leah and I curled up defensively on the couch in the lounge room, Dad yelling and pointing—we'd borrowed the car and I'd trashed it. Leah took the rap for me silently.

I didn't realize I was such a brat. It seemed vastly different from her end, looking from within Leah's world. Shit.

"Try. Let's try. I never tried, not really. Shit, you are my sister."

The pride I clung to had slid away. My eyes moistened and I fought to suppress the contortions of my mouth.

Leah's voice sounded cracked and gnarled.

"I know you think I was Mum's favorite, but it wasn't like that. She was the only thing keeping me safe."

"Safe from what?"

"The pain of those damn fights. Sometimes, I wished they'd kill each other and get it over with."

There was no way I'd ever forget the years of our parent's battles, loud and ferocious, night after night. I knew now it wasn't me alone that bore the scars of our parent's constant fury.

"Me too."

Leah raised her head slightly.

I gazed at her moist red face "I wish you hadn't been so keen to blab about what I was supposedly up to. Half of it was garbage, you know."

"Gypsy, I felt sick thinking what could be happening to you. You were climbing out windows and I imagined the worst. Honestly, I couldn't stand it. I wanted to protect you, not blame you…when I think about all those wasted years when we were enemies."

"Oh." I blew out a breath. Her shoulders came forward. She leaned in to hug me and our heads bumped together. She laughed a crazy, stupid laugh, and together, we did that weird crying and laughing thing, sputtering and stammering. We'd reached some sort of watershed moment, undefined and unstable, but there nonetheless.

After what seemed like an hour, but was probably only a minute or two, the door squeaked open. Renee must have come back with her spoils from the canteen.

"Look, Mum!"

There stood Renee, grinning from ear to ear, her hand inside that of her father's. I'd forgotten how tall he was. He was standing just inside the room grinning stupidly, fair hair falling over his forehead, eyes flicking between Leah and me. I swiped the moisture from my eyes, conscious of my sister perched next to me on the narrow bed, her back to him.

Leah turned her face to within an inch of mine. "What the hell is *he* doing here?" Her voice was a gravelly whisper, her frown a deep line of trenches. This was obviously not a happy family reunion.

"I wanted to talk to you, Leah. Renee told me Gypsy was in the hospital, so when you weren't home, I thought..." His back stiffened as the realization flickered across his face. He clicked that his timing was all wrong and he would cop Leah's full flood of fury.

"Let's talk about this outside." Her voice was low, threatening. As she got off the bed, her lips were pressed together and her eyes were hard. I knew that look—God help him.

"Come on, that's it for one day." She actually leaned over to plant an unexpected dry kiss on my cheek. "Renee, let's go."

Renee rushed over to give me a kiss, throwing her arms around my neck, bringing reminders of happy days.

"See you soon, Gypsy, love you."

Leah pushed past Paul to get out of the room. In

an instant, they were gone. I felt bewildered, drained, and yet strangely enough, contented. Maybe, just maybe, Leah and I would be able to tolerate each other more than we ever had.

*****

Aaron strained as he hauled her into the warehouse. If he hadn't hit her so hard with that crowbar she could have walked herself in. Finally, he managed to drag her onto the old mattress in the storeroom. She was breathing, but hadn't woken for a while now. He thought he'd wacked her in the torso when he pulled the van over to shut her up, but now he could see clumps of blonde hair sticking to her stained features, so he must somehow have caught her face. His lips parted as he brushed his fingers across her face. It was beautiful even when dirtied and bloodied. It would heal; she just needed a bit of time.

He covered her with a blanket and tried getting some water into her, but as he poured from the bottle into her mouth, it just dribbled down the side of her face. He'd managed a quick trip to Carlton, scaring the crap out of the ugly cow's niece. It had been a bit of a giggle, but he had hoped she'd get in the car. Gypsy would have suffered and squirmed over that one. Right now though, he needed to make a list. There were things to do. He'd probably need his old car back and some new license plates from Stewie.

He stood and looked down at her as she stirred, murmuring quietly. She was his and he was hers. All they needed was his baby boy and they'd be a family.

She slowly turned toward him, her eyes opening a crack and she shook her head from side to side, as she registered where she was.

"You! You *bastard*, where am I?" She blinked rapidly, lifting her head off the pillow to look around.

"Our new place, you like it?"

"Oh, my God, you psycho, don't kill me!"

She pressed her fists to her head. Chin trembling, her eyes bulged.

He covered his ears as she started screaming, a barbaric high-pitched wail. It wasn't meant to go like this. He'd been sure her eyes would mist over when she saw him, understanding the hope and promise of their new future together.

"Take me *home*! They'll be looking for me…" Her face contorted.

The pitch of her scream pierced him. He couldn't stand it—she sounded like Tiran, not a fresh start at all. The tangle of thoughts in his head was screeching, overwhelming.

Tiran nagging him screeching, her face contorted in ugliness as she asked him what was going on with him? What the hell was he thinking? The smell of poisonous smoke as he ran into the front yard dragging Christie behind him. Holed up in his room, face down on the bed, pounding the pillow as the knocks, and pleading voices reverberated through the door.

"Shut up! *Shut the fuck up*!" He felt a vein pulsing in his neck as he raged at her. Her head fell back onto the pillow, eyes closed.

He'd been excited when he'd found the report in her bag. They had so much in common. She knew the cops were up to dodgy shit, too, and she had proof. Now she was crazy, and there was no way of talking to her until she calmed down.

He had to get away, because her wails were

seeping into his bones. He ran out to the car, started the engine, and reversed at speed to get out of there.

*****

They'd been on the freeway for a few minutes and the rolling of the car and the slight swaying of their bodies meant a momentary lull in the conversation. Connor tried Aaron again on the phone, but it went straight to voicemail. He clenched his jaw, rubbing his right hand over his left arm, which was locked at the elbow from his hold on the steering wheel. Reining in his emotions, the loss, guilt and anger, was a strain. He wondered how much longer he could keep it up.

Ian turned to Connor. "Let's talk. Now you can tell me who Jeremy O'Connell is."

"A family friend."

"A family friend's name is on the Bedford van, what a fucking coincidence." Ian started rubbing at the tomato stained shirt with a serviette, the fat under his chin wobbling.

"Mum and Dad left the factory to us in the will. We've kept it on, had trouble selling it."

"So that's where we're going? What does that have to do with this Jeremy bloke?" Ian's fingers moved from the stain to the window, fingers tapping the glass with a barely contained annoyance.

"Like I said, he's a family friend. His business was down the road from Dad's factory. Dad borrowed his cars sometimes. They both liked working on them."

His words hung in the air, filling the car, waiting to be inspected and examined.

"So what the fuck are you not telling me?"

"I don't know. I've thought about this for a while.

He's a regular bloke. This isn't something he's capable of, or I didn't think he was. He's like a son to me." Avoiding eye contact, Connor swallowed hard as he flicked on the indicator.

"Who is?" Ian's voice was louder.

"My nephew, Aaron, I think he was the driver of the van that night."

"*Fu-uck*. Reardon, are you for real?"

"We'll find out. I have to at least consider it—a woman's life is on the line."

"Your nephew? The one you took in as a kid? Holy shit."

"Yeah…"

From the corner of his eye, he saw Ian was staring at him slack jawed. Connor couldn't look back at him, didn't want to see his partner's shock. He hadn't wanted to tell him in the first place, but there it was. Glad to be driving, he continued focusing straight ahead.

"Have you told anyone else? Like the chief?"

"No." Connor said in a low tone, his shoulders curled into his chest.

"Someone upstairs needs to know. They've been running around like blue-assed flies. Those reports she took are in the open and they've got the low down on the anti-corruption hearings in there— names, places, suspects."

"What do I tell them? By the way, Chief, I think my nephew killed someone, maybe more than one. I know it might be a bit rough for the department, and I don't have any proof, but I'll get it. I'm all over it."

"Why the hell not?"

Connor gripped the steering wheel so hard his knuckles went white. "Don't be an idiot, Robbo. For a start, the Chief is spitting blood about the reports she smuggled out. He's looking for a head on a pike and it's not going to be mine. Plus, I'm not turning a blood relative in without proof. What's with you, anyway? You've been weird for weeks."

Ian Robson flinched, the tic in his eye flicking madly.

Connor wondered what had gotten into Ian lately. He hadn't been himself. Something was wrong, very wrong, but now was not the time to ask.

"You realize you're in for the fall of a fucking lifetime?"

"What I need is evidence. If we get that, I'll know what to do."

"I'm glad *you* will." Ian rubbed his hand across his mouth, set grimly in a straight line.

Connor turned into a road marked by a service station on the corner, the wide street lined with factories. Silently, they pulled into the driveway of a deserted warehouse. Beyond a sagging chain wire fence was a wide concrete path, cracked with weeds poking through, a large red and white *For Sale* sign, partially obscured by a large bush.

"This it?" said Ian as Connor parked the car at the main entrance, a wooden door with faded blue paint, worn and peeling at the corners.

Connor's heart was racing. He lifted the door handle and opened the car door. He walked through dewy weeds to the blue door. He paused at a window, its dark panes misted over. He remembered his father here, surrounded by car parts, wiping the sweat from his forehead with an old rag. As Connor looked down, he saw rubbish strewn across the path. Soggy newspapers were piled up by the front door. No signs of life. Ian's usual jocular manner had deserted him as he stepped up next to Connor.

"You have a key?" whispered Ian. Connor had slid the gun out of its holster. The safety was off.

Connor reached up to slide the key into the lock. He levered the door open without a sound. The air was musty and stale, the silence thick. They crept across the concrete floor by the light filtering in through dirty old windows. They had their weapons up as they approached the center of the empty, cavernous room. Nothing. Connor recognized a threadbare old chair, rickety brown filing cabinets. As they quietly stepped through a large doorway ahead, their footsteps echoed, the only sound in the seemingly abandoned factory.

Ian nudged a door open with his forearm and it swung before bouncing back an inch.

Connor felt a surge of adrenaline. The room, an old storage room, was gloomy, and smelled dank and stale. His eyes registered the form beneath a stained woolen blanket, slumped on an old mattress. Ian kneeled beside the lifeless figure and peeled back the blanket to reveal a slim, lifeless frame turned on its side. Her blood spattered face was half covered by blonde gluey hair. The woman's hands were tied with electrical wire. Connor held his breath as Ian pushed two fingers into her neck. She murmured softly.

Ian looked up at Connor, his mouth open. "She's alive."

*****

7

I'd managed to shut the bathroom door behind me and stumble back to bed, and as I eased back onto the mattress, I heard another broadcast playing in the background.

"In breaking news, Joanne Seyers has been found alive at an abandoned factory in Western Melbourne. She has been rushed to the hospital, where she is in a serious but stable condition. A statewide manhunt is underway for the perpetrator. We'll update you as this breaking story unfolds…"

I punched my fist in the air. *I told you we'd get him, and we got him.* I felt a rush, a load off my mind and knew that her brother and parents were beyond relief. *Thank God for your persistence, Renee. Thank you, Connor. Take that, faceless bastard. We're coming for you next.*

Cheering, I threw a Post-it note into the air. I needed to tell someone, to share my happiness and rejoice. I grabbed my dressing gown from the bottom of the bed and slid it over my shoulders, making a grab for my walking frame where I hiked my slippers onto my feet. I didn't care what I looked like, granny frame or not. I needed to get to the nurse's station for some human contact.

It was a flurry of activity. Staff in uniform squashed into the nurse's station. The fluorescent light cast a glow over their bowed heads as they gazed at charts, conferring in hushed voices. One was on the phone, another was murmuring to an important looking, tall, middle-aged man in a grey three-piece suit.

"They found her! She's *alive!*" My heart drummed in my chest as I threw my arm wide.

As I reached the desk, a red -haired woman on the phone gestured with one finger that she wouldn't be long.

"Sorry?" said a dark haired nurse who had just arrived and decided to give me her attention.

"Joanne! *Joanne Seyers!* The abducted woman, you know, missing, presumed dead. She's alive! They *found* her!" The nurse managed a thin smile.

"Er…that's good, yes, great news. Now, let's get you back to bed. That's enough for one day." She shoved a pen behind her left ear and ushered me with a scooping motion. Great, they were still humoring me. Why weren't they cheering, waving their hands in the air and flashing their pearly whites? How could they just go on with their daily business, not understanding what had just happened and what this meant for Joanne, her family, her friends?

As the nurse started to lead the way to my room, I was mystified at how my voice was falling across the chasm.

"She could have been *killed!*" I said into the empty air. "But she wasn't. They found her, what were the odds they would find her? Seriously, it's a *miracle!*" There might as well have been tumbleweeds drifting down the thinly carpeted corridor for all the attention I was getting.

"Come on now, that's enough excitement for one

day." The nurse's calm voice obviously intended to soothe and encourage me back to bed.

"Okay, okay I'll get back into bed." I shuffled into the room and to the bed, where I felt the rock-hard mattress give just a little. I couldn't wait to get home to the toasty soft familiarity of my own sweet bed, where I could burrow down into its nooks and crannies. Hopefully, it wouldn't be longer than a week until I was discharged. If the patronizing manner of the staff continued for much longer though, I might be tempted to bop someone over the head myself.

The nurse patted the bed with an expectant smile before stepping out. The TV was back to its usual monotonous drone and I pointed the remote at it to switch it off, which took a few tries of waving the bloody thing up and down. Peace and quiet.

I tried to return to my novel, but I had no hope of concentrating on it. My mind was elsewhere, and the dog-eared pages did not contain my usual choice of reading material. It had been the last one on the ward trolley. Beggars shouldn't be choosers.

Instead, I did what I always do when I can't sleep. I turned on the home shopping channel and fired up the laptop hoping the Wi-Fi would work, so I could do some late night online shopping, but I feared I was being overly optimistic. On the screen above, I saw a perfectly made up woman extoling the benefits of a new whizz bang juicer.

I hoped Connor would be back soon so I could congratulate him. I needed to see his face again. I'd grown rather attached to it.

*****

Renee turned behind to see Leah bolt down the hospital corridor at breakneck speed, her manicured pinky pointed at Paul. Even though he was over a foot taller, she showed no sign of backing off, and little consideration for having not only to look, but also point up at him.

Renee hoped they wouldn't fight again, but knew it was inevitable. She closed her eyes for a moment, praying silently that it wouldn't happen. Since the night her father had moved out, Mum had taken swipes at her dad like a cobra, with fangs showing and the venom flowing.

Today is not the day for it, Mum, not today. Gypsy is getting better, so please not now, not ever.

Nevertheless, if her mother intercepted her thoughts, she didn't care. She seemed oblivious and was ready to strike.

"What the hell was that about? Your timing was *crap*! Then, you never cared about anyone else, did you? We both know you couldn't keep it in your pants long enough to stay the course." Leah's hand shook and her nostrils were flaring.

Paul rubbed his red cheek quickly with a knuckled finger. "I thought you'd want to see me," he said, the corners of his mouth pointed downward as he stuffed his left hand into jean pockets too small to contain it.

"Well, you thought *wrong*!" She stood in front of him with her feet planted firmly apart, one hand on her left hip. "What happened? Did Rita realize you're all talk, no action, then? Or did her husband get a bit pissed off when he saw the dirty text messages?"

Paul looked down, jamming his right hand into the other pocket.

Why did they have to do this? Hadn't there been enough

pain already? Please, stop!

"I just thought we could talk, that's all," He scuffed a piece of fluff on the shabby hospital carpet with the toe of his size twelve shoe.

"Well, it's too late to apologize, Paul, too much bloody water under the bridge." She turned away from him and resumed her march, striding ahead. Renee turned and continued walking almost to the end of the corridor, making her the leader of a march to the packed car park. She didn't trust herself to speak, throat choking and blocked off, angry at the unfairness of it all.

"Okay, I get it. Next time I pick up Renee, though, could I at least put my head in and say hello?"

"Maybe," said Leah, her voice low, "I'll think about it. Let's just leave it at that for now, shall we?"

With that, she was off to catch up with Renee, leaving Paul behind in her dust.

"Wait for me! *Renee!*"

Renee looked up at her.

"Does everything have to be a fight? Can't you two go to counselling or something? Gypsy was almost killed. Seriously, Mum..."

Leah looked down, folding a lock of hair behind her right ear.

"I'm sorry, hon, I know, it's hard for all of us. That was a really bad time for him to show up." Leah sighed, her eyebrows gathering, and she rubbed her chest as if pained. "What did Dad want? Is he moving back home?" Renee's eyes gazed up at Leah hopefully.

"*He* might want to, but I need time," said Leah as the automatic doors made way for them.

"Don't think about it too hard, Mum. I miss him."

Renee brushed her fingers across the bottom of her cardigan. "Things could get back to normal one day. You know, with a bit of time."

"I don't know about that. We'll see. He's got some work to do. It's between me, him, and a marriage counsellor now." Leah rummaged through her bag for the keys, pushed on the remote too hard, and ripped the car door open with more force than necessary.

"Get in!" As she shoved the key into the lock, the car doors slammed and with a loud rev of the engine and squeal of tires, they were gone.

*****

8

Most crime scenes gave him some sort of a rush. Connor wasn't sure whether it was a rush of hope for families, or a chance to track down the lowlife that committed the crime, but he usually felt something, even just a glimmer.

Today, he felt *nothing*. Numb, cut off, and completely adrift.

Of course, he figured Aaron was the key. He'd loved him, cared for him, done the best he could, but right now, it meant nothing. He could feel the swelling around his eyes, although he'd checked the mirror this morning; no sign he'd sat on the bottom of the shower last night, elbows on his knees as he wept. In some strange way, he'd thought the water pounding down from the spray would wash it away, but it hadn't.

Now, here he was today at a crime scene based at his father's old factory. Aaron had taken Jo Seyers there and set up his base. His nephew's mind was gnarled and contorted, and there wasn't a damn thing he could do about it, other than keep trying to find him.

Why would he do something like this without an earlier word, a signal?

He knew why, he just couldn't admit it to himself.

As he so often explained to families, people could keep their true motivations secret, especially if they thought someone or something would get in their way. When it happened to his nephew, his own flesh and blood, everything seemed foreign, out of place.

The shock was catching up with him. He staggered back into the present, shaking his head lightly, to continue the motions of collecting evidence and comparing notes with Ian Robson.

"Our buddies from the news station got here in record time," said Ian, as he bent over with trembling hands to seal the last in a series of tightly arranged packets. They were in the storeroom where they'd found Joanna Seyers, and they were sifting through for evidence.

"Yeah." Connor ran his fingers through his hair, sweat tickling his spine.

"Time to get out of here, I think. I'd rather not be around if the chief turns up." Ian's face was encased in a glistening sheen of sweat.

"Maybe. Just give me a few minutes. I need to make a call." Connor walked out of the room, stepping over cameras and tape as he headed to the open space of the front yard. He headed over to a corner between clusters of old bushes, out of sight of the media pack. He massaged his temples and gazed at the tinted windows of the factory next door. After a couple of seconds, he stopped pacing and pulled out his phone.

It answered on the third ring.

"Nathan." Connor paused for a beat and rubbed the back of his neck. "Yeah, Connor. Listen, I need a favor—witness in the hospital, St Vincent's. I need a uniform outside her room. Can you organize it?" He stepped back, placing a hand over his other ear. "Yeah, thanks mate, it's intense right now and the last thing we need is another casualty. Text me when it's sorted, okay?"

As he peered into the street, the squat square van with the rooftop satellite dish pointing to the clouds, announced that the journalists had set up camp. The van door was open and a blond presenter stood in front, microphone at the ready. He leaned over to murmur to a cameraman struggling with the weight on his shoulder. At the front of the old factory, he'd passed a junior constable with hands clasped around a clipboard standing guard behind the blue and white tape, securing entry to the scene. The factory itself was humming with activity. Two technicians in white hooded jumpsuits had been dusting surfaces in the storage room, the blue bristles of their brushes fanning in systematic sweeping movements.

He heard a car pull into the factory driveway. The cameras and reporters bolted for it. A tall man emerged from the passenger seat, unfolding his six foot four frame from the car, his spine a rod of iron. Connor noticed that police chief, Jack Reynolds, was in full uniform and had ditched the usual un-ironed shirt and glasses perched on top of his head. His grey-black hair was seamlessly set, a cap perched on top, authority shining from silver pips on the shoulders of his immaculately prepared uniform.

The media pack shoved microphones underneath the chief's chin, jostling for position. He hooked his hands in front of him, clearing his throat loudly before speaking with a raspy, resonant timbre.

"I'm proud that the combined power of Victoria Police, including the swift efforts of investigators, has led to the successful location of Joanne Seyers, who is in a serious but stable condition. Obviously, the focus for her family is full recovery while we identify the perpetrator. I'm confident that given our progress to date, this case will be fully resolved as a matter of extreme priority. Thank you." His palms came up, signaling the end of his statement. As he stepped away, the questions came rapid-fire, gaining in intensity.

"What about the perpetrator? Could he strike again?"

"How was the victim found? What was the process used to find her?"

"Who were the investigators? What's the next step?"

The chief turned, raising his voice in a tone of clipped annoyance. "Ladies and gentlemen, that is our current statement. As more information comes to light, we will update you. We will advise on developments in due course. A press conference is scheduled for later this evening. Thank you for your cooperation." His long legs carried him away from the pack. As he reached the tape, the constable nodded at him, a solemn expression on his young face.

The chief ducked through the doorway, scanning the knot of personnel, looking for the largest group. He found Ian sealing a cardboard box with tape. Connor watched from the front yard as Jack Reynolds's back disappeared through the door and reluctantly headed inside after him. Better to face a small volcano now than wait until the anger had peaked into a size ten earthquake style face rip.

Ian felt a presence behind him and turned around,

tape poised mid-air. "Sir." His gaze shifted as Connor entered the room.

"Robson, I hear you were a key player. Nice work." The chief pulled in a deep breath, shoulders back and chest out.

Ian preened. "The main mover and shaker was Reardon. He got us here."

Connor shuffled across to stand next to the chief, and watched as his head turned to look down at him.

"Ah, Connor." He extended a hand, his grip firm and cold. "The reports?"

"No sign. We're following up leads on the perp."

The chief frowned and lowered his hand. "Witnesses? The owners of the property have been interviewed?" His green eyes were lasers, his smile forced.

"Deceased. The property's been vacant for some time." Connor's finger twitched and he bit down on his bottom lip.

"I see. Interview the landlord. We need this guy's movements and fast."

"Well, you see—" Connor could feel the familiar heat rising in his chest, and he scraped at it through his shirt. His damn hives were playing up again, not the time to show his unease. He could feel the raised lumps and red dots forming across his chest and Connor pulled his hand away. "You're looking at him."

Chief Reynolds look shifted to Connor's chest. "What the hell are you talking about, Reardon?" A frown threatened his narrow set eyes and he crossed his arms. "Who am I looking at?"

Connor pulled on his earlobe. "This is our factory. My parents left it to me and my sister"

"Jesus *Christ*, Reardon, you're not serious?"

"Well…" Connor wondered how long it would take for the storm to pass.

"Do you have any idea what this means? Once the media gets their grubby hands on this…" Jack rubbed his face with an open hand, as if rubbing thoughts of scandal as far away as possible. "I've scheduled a press conference for tonight. Be there."

"But sir—"

The chief took a step forward, pointing a hairy finger at Connor. "St Kilda Road Headquarters. Eight pm. We'll meet in my office an hour before." He looked across at Robson. "What's your knowledge of this?"

Ian paled, tucking his shirt back in to his trousers. "Er…well, it all happened pretty fast."

"It could get messy. If you thought you were under pressure before, you were kidding yourselves. Miss the conference and kiss your careers goodbye." He stormed out, ducking slightly to get through the doorway.

Ian gave Connor a sideways look. "Fucking hell, Connor, I'm out of here." Ian grabbed the box from the top of a filing cabinet and tucked it under his left arm.

"There's someone I need to check on. See you at the press conference."

"Yeah, I'll get a lift with Tom the techie." Mouth set, Ian clomped out, his hair flopping over his ears with each heavy step.

Connor left the factory, walking quickly around the media scrum, which was thankfully distracted by Ian. Head down, he brushed sweaty hair away from his vision. There was something, or rather *someone* he wanted to take care of.

9

The dark haired man sat in the car several doors down from the crime scene. He looked down at his brown shoes, shuffling them as he waited. The car was comfortable and he waited for the right moment. He had to be sure the detective had left the crime scene and the media pack had thinned before venturing back in for a more thorough search.

It fucking well had to be in there somewhere.

When he'd heard the report was in the air, read by not only Joanne Seyers' dumb fucking administrator, but also that dirt bag Aaron, he had drunk more than his usual couple of glasses.

His head lifted and he watched as the detective walked into the street. He headed over to his car, unlocking it and climbing in. The man waited as the car started up, lights on and it took off and turned at the end of the street, out of sight.

Things weren't great at home. The old girl had picked up on his squirming misery, pushing him for answers he wouldn't give, not a chance in hell. Why couldn't she understand that he'd taken risks for her. They needed the money. He wasn't a complete fucking bastard like she said he was.

Eighteen months ago, Rachel had lost nearly twenty hours of work per week. When it all happened, they'd figured they could make up the shortfall somehow, but the financial pressure got to both of them. The yelling, the dramatic scenes had drained him.

So when the opportunity presented itself, he took it. He was surveying the crime scene and it was quiet, not a soul around. He heard a couple of them in the other room. The scene was almost deserted, a large amount of cash, over eighty grand. No one had seen him take it, besides, it was such a small amount it wouldn't make any difference. Who would miss a couple of grand in the scheme of eighty, and a pinch of dope from a large bag? No one that's who.

It had paid a few bills, taken the pressure off for a while.

However, once the money dried up, the screaming matches began again. She thought he was having an affair and if she wasn't hurling abuse at him, he might have snorted at the ridiculousness of her accusation. They'd been at each other's throats for so long that when another opportunity to nab some cash fell into his lap, he took it.

When he heard about the police administration girl going missing, his gut had dropped. The feeling within his chest, the terror, tugging at him, surging and buzzing, became his own private agony. He figured it would subside in time, but it didn't. Maybe his name wasn't on the damn internal affairs fucking report, but maybe it was.

If it was, not only was his career over, but his marriage too.

He'd heard about the retired cops, the divorced cops, the depressed ones all on the list. Most of them would probably end up as tragic suicides, an all too convenient gun to the head. He'd be fucked if that would happen to him.

If he could just find the report, the mess could be contained early, nipped in the bud.

He pushed the car door open and got out, pointing the remote to lock it.

He'd perfected the art of blending in. He had his partner figured out. They had been working together for years now and he didn't have a damn clue. He headed back inside. He'd find the report. He had to, because there was no other choice.

*****

I'd had enough of pajamas. Interesting phenomena that—after spending my life wishing I could spend my life in pajamas, when it actually happened, I was much more motivated by the concept of dressing myself and wearing regular clothes.

Leah had brought in a few things from home, which helped, but nothing could ever make the damn hospital room as comfortable as my flat. I missed my aquarium with fish that I'd practically taken out a small loan to buy, my purple couch with the worn out butt groove patch. I missed my computer, my stereo, and all the little things that made it home.

Today, I would walk around the hospital ward and smile in at my fellow residents, dazzling them with my progress regardless of their looks of curiosity, and in some cases, resentment. I had graduated from a senior citizen's walking frame to a walking stick, which was much more dignified. Strangely enough, in the past, I'd often gazed at walking sticks with a sense of admiration. Perhaps I found myself the user of said stick because of my too-frequent envy.

The blinds were up and rays of winter sunlight streamed into the room. I was starting to feel almost human again. My mission for the day was to walk around and cheer up fellow patients, give them hope as they witnessed my walk of triumph. I needed to see regular people, not hospital patients, going about their daily lives. I wanted to see families and partners kissing and hugging, talking about everyday mundane events, living their lives. I'd had enough of the injured and infirm waiting for recovery and discharge. I wasn't good at waiting. I'd been psyching myself up for today's walk for at least an hour prior, and as I stood beside the bed, I gave my walking stick an optimistic bounce, the rubber reverberating reassuringly on the hospital tiles. I caught it with what I told myself was a jaunty movement, reminiscent of Gene Kelly in Singing in the Rain. I felt a slow grin take hold, a sign that life was on the way back, almost to normal, if such a thing existed.

The nurse's station was about a hundred meters from my door, so the staff knew exactly when I left my room and could stop me to ask a question or usher me back to bed. The way I was feeling, I decided that wouldn't be a problem. I was ready for an argument, feeling strong hund confident. If one more nurse reminded me to be careful of overstimulation, maybe I wouldn't restrain myself from over stimulating *them* with a verbal lashing or worse.

Although my steps were slow and marked by a slight limp at that moment, I was thankful that my left arm and leg did as commanded and would actually propel me forward. I didn't have complete feeling in either limb, but I knew this was just around the corner, considering the relatively short time it had taken me to get from zero almost to well.

I opened the door and my ears were assaulted by the unexpected sounds of life, a swirling mass of noise and bodies crammed into a tiny space. Buzzers were buzzing, phones ringing, fluorescent lights lighting and staff conferring. I shuffled past without looking at them, my face hot. I resisted the urge to scratch, not wanting to raise a hand to my face and attract unwanted attention. As it had throughout my childhood and adolescence, my height often meant a sting of self-consciousness. Gestures made by the tall and gigantic seemed more visible. As I turned the corner, I lifted my head, proud at least of the fact that I was dressed and upright. A bright pink headscarf covered the bristles on my head and I had, with a rush of spontaneity, stuck a purple flower behind my ear. A flourish of insouciance, it made a statement that despite the odds, I was still alive. I punched in the code to exit the ward, four short high beeps until the door yielded with a satisfying long blare, followed by a click. My strength had returned and I shouldered the heavy door open, onward and outward. I peered out through the corridor's floor to ceiling windows, watching the figures chatting and laughing in the courtyard a few floors below. The greenery was bending in the wind, and although it was winter, I felt the surge of energy that was life.

Eventually, I reached the elevator. Yet another bell

chimed and I stepped in. Staring at the closed doors, I remembered hearing somewhere that a rebellious patient once entered an elevator facing its occupants and stared to watch their reactions. I wasn't quite sure I was up to that level of cockiness, but I was almost back to full battery, my cheekiness level and sense of humor brimming.

I felt the floor drop just before we landed at ground level. I looked down, twirling the tip of the walking stick to gauge its weight and rhythm. Hell, if I were up to it I would have busted out a soft shoe shuffle. I stepped into the corridor and heard the throng of people in the cafeteria before I reached my destination. As I shuffled down the corridor to reach the hub, I saw the bright lights in the glass cabinets displaying muffins, cakes, and other niceties. My mouth was watering for the right reason today: hunger. It was peak coffee hour, and I queued up to place my order. The woman at the register was wide, the stringy belt on her black apron cutting a welt into her middle.

"What would you like, love?"

"Ah, latte with two, please, take-away." I surveyed the double-door fridge stocked with drinks of every possible kind. A sign behind her advertised ice cream, and the blackboard beside her hocked the day's specials.

I pulled a bill out of my pocket and handed it over. "What the hell, I'll have a banana muffin as well." I heard the clack of the register drawer and opened my hand out to catch the change, reveling in the mundaneness of it all.

Her dark brown curls bounced as she handed me

the coins. "Latte with two and a banana muffin, no worries. Name for the order?"

"Gypsy." My name rolled around on my tongue, one of a kind.

"Okay, love, we'll call you when it's ready." She tilted her head to seek out the next customer. I walked over to a table and sank down into a plastic white chair. I checked my watch twice before my name was called. I held the paper cup tightly, and began my shuffling journey back to the elevator. As I hobbled along the corridor, heads above random nametags smiled at me in what seemed to be encouragement for being upright, soldiering on. I stopped to admire the stream of sunshine pouring through the windows and hunched by the closest pane, closing my eyes as the beams hit my skin. I imagined myself on the beach, reading a book with a drink at the ready. The bubble burst, perforated by a particularly loud conversation, so resentfully I shuffled off again.

Back on my floor, I shouldered the ward door open. To catch my breath, I leaned against the sprawling desk. My head rose, peripheral vision registering the pale blue of a police uniform outside my door. I shuffled with uneven steps, my slippers grazing the carpet as I approached the trespasser. He peered at an internal window, not realizing I was there, before transferring his scrutiny to my eyes.

"Hello." His voice was deep and gruff. In a heartbeat, I registered black raised lettering on a gold breastplate: *Junior Const. Millar.*

"Yes, *madam?*"

Something about the syrupy emphasis irked me. "You could start by explaining why you're outside my room."

He shifted uncomfortably. "Ah, I can't really talk about an open investigation." He looked down at the reflection shining in his black sturdy shoes.

"You can't talk about it? You can't talk about two attempted murders from a *slime ball*?" There was no other reason he could be there than to protect me from the faceless reptile that hurt me. My eyes narrowed, and I lifted my shoulders to yank at my shirt cuff almost ripping it out at the seams. "Can you talk about the bastard that abducted Joanne Seyers? I wonder if *she's* talking." I snorted, forcing back the urge to shake the stick at him.

"I'm sorry. You could take it up with the investigating officer." He spoke at a low volume, his face a standoff, like a bulletproof mask.

"I would if he bothered to show himself. All care, no responsibility, right?" As heads turned our way, I backed off a little, releasing my breath. He shot a sideways look and moved aside as I retreated, his heels clicking together.

Turning the handle, I backed in through the door using my heel to pry it open. My back creaked as I lowered my weary body to the bed. Lifting my chin, I looked to the unadorned bone-white ceiling scanning the pictures within. What was Connor doing right at this very moment? I sought him out, but he had shielded himself as if with armor plate. No chance. His empathy and lack of reaction to my abilities struck me in blinding recognition. I hadn't received any sense earlier that this was the case, but now I knew for certain. He wasn't just distracted, he was shutting me out, and he damn well knew it. While he may not be able to confront his own abilities, they were real, and sturdy enough to block curious intruders.

I flicked on the TV, where the police chief's stern face advised of an upcoming press conference.

What was Connor doing? Would he ever come back? I wish he'd let me in, allow me to crack open the vault of secrets and expose them. I was stymied by my body, although the mind was willing, aggravated by my lack of input in this investigation. The combined effects of a disobedient body were taking their toll, piece by piece. I tapped my finger on the side of the bed, and swore under my breath, hoping to release my pent up frustration.

I pounded the table wondering if it would break. It held, spinning away slowly.

Goddamn, I couldn't take much more of this.

If Connor didn't show up soon, I'd be forced to make a break for it.

*****

Aaron blew the air out from his cheeks hoping to gain control, glad to be out of there and on the road. The lights from oncoming traffic shone like a flurry of lanterns as he gripped the steering wheel tightly.

He turned on speakerphone, plugging in the number he had rung a thousand times before, and listened as it rang out through the cabin.

"Hello?"

"Tiran, it's me. I'm sorry about what happened…"

"What the hell is going *on*? You just disappeared—where *are* you?" Her voice was high pitched and rushed, the words tumbling over each other.

"Don't worry for now, I rang to warn you something's up."

"What the hell? Of course, something's up! You pushed me over. My face is *purple*! If you had any balls, you'd come back and face me. Aaron, *what* is going on? If this is another crazy idea, I swear…"

He felt intensely cold, his throat dry, legs restless. "It was an accident. I'm sorry, I really am. I'll be back to see you and the boy soon." He'd pulled the car over. His head was tilted in a side-to-side rhythm. He needed to talk to Stewie. Although the guy could be brainless, he'd at least have an opinion on this, on the next step, what to do with the explosive report.

"Tiran, we've had our moments, but I have proof this time. For real."

"Proof of *what*?" Aaron heard the pitch of her voice rise at the end, slowly spinning a tornado of near hysteria.

"An internal affairs report and I reckon I'm the only one that has it. Proof the cops are dirty—names of suspects, dates it's all here, *evidence*. Some of them got their hands filthy stealing the crime scene stash: cash, weapons, drugs. I want you to write these names down. If anything happens to me…"

"You're scaring me …*stop*!"

"This is real. I'm not kidding around. If you believe nothing else, believe this. These are the scumbags, the bent ones. Go get some paper and write these names down." He bounced a foot, and stroked an eyebrow.

Hurry up, Tiran, goddamn it, hurry the hell up!

He heard the clatter as she dropped the phone to go searching for the post-it notes they kept on the bench.

"Okay, I'm back. Aaron, you know this is weird, right?" she sounded slightly out of breath.

"If any of these people contact you, run. Hang up, slam the door in their face, whatever. They might know by now I have the report, and pay you a visit…"

"Seriously? What the…"

"Write down these names." He felt dizzy, his chest tightening. It was all starting to catch up with him. Thank God, he got to her first.

"Okay, okay, hang on." He could almost hear her concentrating, and imagined her on the other end— brow furrowed, tongue protruding slightly as she scribbled down the names.

He'd memorized them and began reciting.

"David Atkinson. Pete Reynolds. Ian…"

He heard the doorbell ring in the background, loud and musical.

"I've got to go, there's someone at the door."

"What? *Who?*" he rubbed at his upper lip. "Keep writing, Tiran."

"I don't know who, but I don't think it's a cop. Dark hair, blue car, no uniform. Ring me back."

Before he could say another word, the dial tone pulsed loudly in his ear. She'd hung up. He hoped those two names were enough.

*****

The dark haired stranger turned the car off in the drive and sat for a minute. Through the window, he could see her in the lounge. She had left the curtains open with the lights on.

When the curtain twitched, he knew she had seen him. He took a deep breath and got out of the car. It squeaked and bounced from the release of the weight as he stood. He wasn't sure what she knew, but he'd soon find out. As he stepped onto the front porch, she opened the door. Curly damp hair clung to her face, and she pulled a strand out of her mouth as she looked at him blankly, waiting for him to explain who he was.

"Yes?" He heard the edge in her voice.

"Tiran?"

"Yes."

"Can I come in?"

"What's this about?" She had obviously been cleaning. The front of her yellow floral top was wet, and her hands were damp and wrinkled.

"I need some information." He shoved his foot into the door, and then pushed past her to gain entry.

"What?" Her voice was loud and shrill. "This is my *house!* I can't believe you just—" She chased after him, one slipper sliding off her foot on the way.

"What's this?" He had reached the kitchen and held a blue Post-it note in his hand above her head.

He saw droplets of sweat forming on her forehead. She backed away, her hands feeling for the smooth contours of the kitchen door with her fingers. He needed to strike before she could get the thing open and curl her fingers around a knife.

"I want to know where you got your information," he growled, his feet thumping as he stepped closer to her.

"None of your business. I'm calling the police." Tiran's eyes were hard, neck muscles taut.

"You stupid bitch." His lip curled in a snarl as he brought his right hand up to her rounded shoulders. With his left hand, he pulled out sickly yellow plastic gloves and she froze, rooted to the spot.

"Get away from me before I call the cops. *Get out of my house!*" Her voice was ear splitting, and as she pushed off from her back foot, he strengthened his hold on her shoulder. The phone was only a couple of feet away.

"Where are the reports? This list...where did it come from?"

"What reports? I don't know what you mean!"

"Where are they?"

"I don't know!"

Something inside him ruptured, sending acidic bile rearing up to burn him.

He grabbed her throat, and the warmth as her body left the ground surged through his fingers. A kernel of fury germinated in the pit of his stomach. Her legs bashed against the wall. She grabbed at his face, fingers outstretched.

Holding on tightly, he listened to the gurgling and waited until she stopped. He slowly released his grip, and she dropped like a bag of ball bearings, landing with a thud before her limbs spilled at awkward angles on the floor, mouth open, glassy eyes unseeing. He wiped his hands on his pants and stormed into the kitchen. There he ripped open doors from cabinets, dislodged drawers, smashing closets. It had to be here somewhere. He stormed from room to room, spilling cupboards, yanking drawers, eyes scanning frantically.

The baby in the bedroom was screaming, his chubby hands grabbing the sides of the cot, a wet pink tongue protruding above two pearly buds of teeth.

"Fuck," he whispered to himself, the boy's screaming a ringing vibration shaking his skull.

He stormed down the hallway. Stepping over the lifeless form, he made for the front door. As it slammed behind him, he stood on the front porch and scanned the darkness, planning his next move.

10

Five more minutes and he would be with Bailey. The lights from an oncoming car flashed past, a lighthouse in the gloom. Aaron hadn't meant to hurt Tiran. It was an accident. He wondered how she'd greet him after four days away—more than likely with an avalanche of blame, shame, and regret. He really didn't need more yelling and screeching. She wasn't the sharpest tool in the shed and if he told her he wanted to take Bailey out for a drive, a father and son bonding session, she'd be satisfied. He forced his foot down on the accelerator, feeling his body roll as he took the corner hard, tires squealing.

Aaron drove for what felt like hours but was only a few minutes, feeling the car roll around the corners, propelling him, carrying him to his home. His seat bobbed as he arrived and he felt the vibrations as the engine idled. He turned off the ignition key and looked up, waiting for the first twitch of the shades.

The windows were lit up, curtains open, illuminating familiar territory. He waited for the usual routine when he arrived home, which didn't come. Usually Tiran would either open the front door or have the porch light on when she heard his van pull up.

He stepped up to the front porch, feeling the icy

air whip across his cheeks. Bailey's screams seared their way through the door.

Which meant that either something had happened to Tiran or she'd left Bailey alone? Much as he resented her, he knew that wasn't possible.

His posture stiffened feeling the rigidity in his muscles. He shook his head.

"No, no, not Tiran, not her," he heard the shakiness in his voice.

Who did this? When? Why?

In the depths of numbness, he realized the jeopardy. Tiran had said someone was at the front door, a bloke in a blue car with dark hair.

Some faceless cop identified only in the report. The list he read out to Tiran.

Holy fucking hell.

Of course, he'd be the prime suspect, the first one the cops would turn to as the bad guy. He was a bad guy. He had grabbed Jo off the street to start a new life he didn't expect anyone to understand. Some dodgy pig was taking advantage, but not for long. He had gotten pretty good at tracking people down.

He took a breath in and pulled out the key. The scream wasn't a cry of need or hunger, but one of terror. It permeated the house, seeping into the walls. He hadn't heard Bailey howl like that, not ever.

As he pushed the front door open, the screaming became louder, more intense. Looking to the left, he saw her collapsed on the hallway floor. He ran to Tiran, landing on his knees heavily.

"Tiran!" He fumbled for a pulse. Her skin felt cold and foreign. Aaron held his head in his hands, wailing as he rocked slightly.

"Why did you let him in? Why?" He slowly stood

on rubber legs to make his way to Bailey's bedroom. He couldn't ignore the screaming any longer. As he stomped through the hallway, he bashed on the walls with a curse.

Seeing his father, Baily lifted his hands up, eyes red, begging to be picked up.

He picked Bailey up, realized he needed a nappy change and grabbed clothes from the cupboards, stuffing them manically into a blue and green cloth bag, leaving the legs of a playsuit hanging out as he searched for a bottle and nappies. Drawers were flung across the room. Whoever it was, they'd been looking for something and needed it in a hurry.

Like a smuggled report on police corruption.

After hurriedly changing Bailey's nappy, he flung the strap of the bag over his shoulder and stepped around the drawers. He had to get moving and fast. He stomped down the hallway.

He wouldn't be getting the department involved, DHS could go to hell. Once they knew, Bailey would be lost to him forever. He didn't need stuffed shirts poking their nose in where it wasn't needed. Bailey belonged with him and Jo. Once the department found out he'd smoked weed months ago, he'd never see his son again. Bailey was coming with him.

Aaron paused for one last look before stepping over Tiran, whose open lips were changing color. He focused his thoughts on the here and now. He wiped one hand down his dirty jeans and made for the front door. Slamming it behind him, he adjusted his clothes, which could probably do with a change. He'd had other more important things on his mind. He felt the hairs on the nape of his neck stiffen. Time to strap Bailey in, change over the license plates and head back to Laverton. He'd been delaying the inevitable, but his hand had been forced. It was time for action, to return Connor's calls.

*****

The stark rays pierced a gap in the curtains, the prisms waking her. Renee opened her eyes slowly, lashes batting her cheek. She looked around, wondering what was different. Listening carefully as she licked her lips, she felt her scalp prickle. Although there was no one here, she knew she was being watched. Something was wrong, very wrong. She lifted her arms above the covers, goose bumps forming.

There was a pinging, an alarm bell going off inside, thoughts intruding that didn't belong, malicious, lingering pictures of hurting, torturing, and smashing. The curly haired dirty man smashed a window at the side of a house, climbing through, brushing himself down. A dead woman lay hideously contorted on the ground as a baby screamed; sitting in a dirty smelly house talking to a man who looked like he needed a shower, making quiet evil plans.

What was *wrong* with her? She threw back the covers, padding out of the room on slippered feet.

The images persisted as Renee pulled open bedroom drawers, selecting clothes for the day. Thoughts like this originated from one source alone: her aunt. The pictures persisted, forcing their way in. They had weight and force, and she struggled to understand.

Padding downstairs, she poured her breakfast cereal into a bowl and sat at the kitchen table, hoping the mundane and routine would help, but the pictures persisted. Her mind flashed scenes at her, flicking through at the speed of light.

It was the man, the creepy man that followed her.

A van was parked by the side of the road. The man was kicking the tires, his limbs flailing wildly, entire body jolting as he lashed out. Realization struck. The house the scary man was breaking into belonged to her aunt.

That horrible, creepy, horrible man was searching for Gypsy, hunting her, sniffing her out, tracking her down.

Oh God.

The spoon fell, clanging onto the tiles. Milk spilled across the kitchen bench. Renee ran for her bedroom, where she rummaged through the wardrobe for her shoes. Sandals, sneakers, and boxes were sent catapulting onto the carpet beside her.

She paused for a moment and looked at the mountain of shoes. There was no way she could reach the hospital to warn Gypsy. Mum was out at her second job, Dad wouldn't be here for a couple of hours, and she had only a sketchy knowledge of the route.

The spark of an idea formed, but could she do it? She at least had to try, knowing that if she didn't, Gypsy might be hurt again.

They had gotten into a routine. They usually only shared thoughts when touching, and always when they were in the same room, so this would be a first.

The best place to try out her new abilities would be where she felt the most comfortable and relaxed: her bedroom.

Pushing the wardrobe door back, she dodged the shoes, flung back the covers, and lay across the pink flannelette sheets, staring at the ceiling. She turned toward the window and snuggled down, tucking her left hand under the feather pillow.

Renee closed her eyes and focused on slowing her breathing. Initiating the process felt like throwing out a line, a rope. When she was talking to Gypsy, sometimes the connection was so strong she could almost see the line, taut and electric, almost humming. With a bird's eye view, she looked over the general area, sensing the hospital's general direction. Finding her way through the surging swirl of pictures flicking at her a mile a minute was tough. She bumped into other people's mental images sometimes and tuned them out, as she located the building, the pale bricks and the visitors loitering outside its entrance reassured her that she was on the right track. She smiled to herself, shuffling further up the bed.

She headed inside the building and ventured up through the floors, past the café, past anxious families huddled together in waiting rooms, and staff conferring with serious looks.

Scanning quickly, she found Gypsy's room on the third floor. Renee settled in the top corner of the room. She saw Gypsy lying on the bed reading a novel. Her face looked relaxed, or at least less strained than the last time she saw her.

Look at that, I don't believe it! She'd done it.

The next task was to get her aunt's attention. Looking at the yellow Post-it notes on the table, she realized these would be perfect. Gypsy loved her Post-it notes. They were plastered all over her flat. They were on the back of the front doors, cupboards, practically wallpaper. What if Renee could make the paper move without any wind? It was an exciting idea, but she wasn't sure how on earth she would do it.

Whatever she did, it had to happen fast.

Her thoughts racing, she focused every ounce of her energy onto moving the notes. Even a small flutter would do it. She took a huge breath and held it, using the momentum to focus. She pushed her energy outwards, fixed and unwavering. With satisfaction, she saw the paper flicker a little, and she let go of her breath in a rush, gasping for air, recovering her pulse to a normal rate.

It had worked better than she could have hoped. The paper flickered, its corners moving even though the window in the room was closed, with no trace of wind. When she saw the flickering pages gaining momentum, flicking faster in the stillness of the hospital room, Renee smiled. Gypsy looked up from her book, her back going ramrod straight.

Seizing the moment, Renee tried to establish a line to her aunt.

Gypsy? Can you hear me? Are you getting this? She saw Gypsy shuffle awkwardly across the bed, closer to the Post-it notes on the table, her mouth hanging open.

Renee? Is that you? Seriously?

Yes, I'm here. I had to talk to you, it's important.

Her aunt's face broke into a toothy grin.

I'm impressed. This sort of thing isn't easy.

Yeah, I know. Renee preened, a smile breaking free and taking hold.

You certainly got my attention. Gypsy's thoughts filled her mind.

I wanted to warn you, Renee's voice was echoing through Gypsy's mind.

Warn me? Gypsy ran her fingers across her mouth, rubbing absentmindedly.

The creepy man is hunting you, stalking you. Renee

grazed fingers across her collarbone. The more she thought about him, the worse she felt, nausea churning.

Gypsy shuddered. Renee felt a chill down her back as she thought about the faceless man tracking her aunt, chasing her.

There's a policeman outside the door.

There is?

Yes, he arrived yesterday. Connor arranged for a guard outside my room. I'll be fine.

Renee pulled the bed coverings more tightly around her body. *He's approached a friend, asking for your address. Don't go home, please don't go home. He'll be there, I know it.*

Renee, calm down. Let the police do their job. I can take care of myself.

This did little to ease Renee's mind. She shook her head. *Gyp, let me talk to Mum. Maybe you can stay with us. Just for a few days, give them a chance to catch this man.*

Renee saw Gypsy's shoulders heave. Renee knew Gypsy longed to be home, but her safety was more important.

All right, Renee, if you are that worried about it, I'll talk to your mum. If she agrees, I'll stay at your place for a bit. But only for a few days—I'm not used to living with my sister. It's been a long time.

Yay! I'll tell Mum tonight. Maybe we'll even come in to see you in person. Renee smiled, her toes curling in satisfaction. She couldn't wait to have her aunt stay with them where she would be safe. With a quick goodbye, she broke the connection and ran downstairs, doing a little dance on the way down. He'd never find her aunt here.

*****

As I rested my head back against the pillow, I thought about Connor, wondering if I was ready for love again. After my split with Mark, I'd decided that I was probably just too difficult to deal with and given up my dream of having children of my own. Leah's comments about finding a man and having children had burned because she'd tapped into my greatest fear. I'd thought Mark was the one and that we'd be together forever and would have a gaggle of beautiful children.

On the night we broke up, I had no idea it was about to happen. After three false alarms, we'd always gotten back together.

The door to my hospital room creaked open bringing me back to the present. Connor had finally shown his handsome face. There he was, staring at my bed with a contemplative look. His hair was tousled and he looked like he had slept in his clothes. The dark shadows under his eyes spoke volumes.

I tried not to be too surly and resentful.

"So, you decided I was worth another visit, did you?" I raised a hand to my head. Thank goodness, I was wearing a scarf today to cover my hair, which was still growing back.

Connor looked at me without blinking. "I'm sorry, Gypsy. I know I said I'd be back soon. The investigation is intense and I've been distracted." He looked down at the floor.

He looked so ashamed that I instantly forgave him. With a face like that, how could I not?

"I missed you," I said, turning my head to look at him.

His head came up sharply and he ventured a smile. "You did?"

"Yes, I did." I smiled at him, and I meant it.

"Oh, er, that's good," he said clearly unsure of where to go from here. He grabbed his earlobe, rubbing it tenderly as he shifted the chair across to my bedside and sat down tentatively.

Now that the coffee date we had so flippantly suggested when we first met was off the table, I wanted to get to know Connor.

"So much for catching up for coffee then, huh?" I tried a small smile, gazing across at him.

Connor smiled back. "Yeah, I guess you never can tell…"

"Have you and Jill been split for long?" My sudden diverting comment was intended to get to know Connor as soon as I could. After my brush with death, who knew how long I'd have with the man. Moreover, if there was one thing I'd learned after my break up with Mark, it was to take opportunities where I could.

He bowed his head. "Almost a year now, but it feels like at least three times that."

"Yeah, I know that feeling. Ten months for me after Mark. The loneliness doesn't go away like I thought it would. Main problem is the regret, shoulda woulda coulda helps no one. Doesn't mean it doesn't hurt like hell though. Sometimes I wonder if I'd done things differently would we still be together."

Connor's eyes came up and he met my gaze. He understood.

"Somehow, I don't think so. Besides, if the cards had played out differently we wouldn't have met." The ghost of a smile flickered across his face.

"Well, that's true. Shame a bash across the head was our second date though." I felt my face heat up.

Shit, maybe he didn't think of a hospital visit as a date at all. Maybe it was all in the line of duty.

What an idiot you are, Gypsy.

He unfolded his frame from the chair and headed over to my bedside where he perched on the right hand side of the bed, taking my hand in his.

His hand was warm, rough, and reassuring.

"I wish you hadn't been attacked either, but we'll work with what we've got."

A rush of heat reached my chest.

"If only…" I said. The damn door creaked open again and the nurse Tina appeared, yet again. The timing of the revolving door of nurses checking my vital signs was taking its toll.

She flicked a glance to Connor and me as he slowly removed his hand from my grip.

"Sorry, time to check your blood pressure again."

The interruption brought me out of my Connor induced reverie and into the present.

"I noticed you sent an officer to guard my room," I said. "It would have been nice to have known before the fact."

"Yeah, I know I should have called first. Investigations can move pretty fast once we get a lead, and I tend to get caught up." He looked down at his phone.

"So what about Renee? The creep followed her home from school, you know that, right?"

"What?" Connor looked pale under his tan.

"Yeah, he found me. How do I protect my niece? Is there anything you can tell me?"

Connor cleared his throat and slowly lifted his chin. "I'll arrange for a patrol car to drive past Renee's home. The perpetrator is still at large and you are the only witness at present. It stands to reason he'll come for you."

"What, in the hospital?" I stared down at my hands, my mouth suddenly dry.

"Stranger things have happened. I would hate for anything to happen to you," said Connor quietly.

Were we having a moment here in hospital? It would be a whole lot better if we were at home. The faceless bastard had a lot to answer for.

"It would be better if you went somewhere safe once you're discharged," said Connor, his brow creasing.

"Now that you mention it, Renee is insistent that I move in with her and my sister when I'm discharged."

"That's good, but I'd feel better if you were further away. Are there any relatives interstate that would take you in for a while?"

"No. I don't see why I should change my entire life for this bastard. I didn't do anything wrong!" I could feel my face flushing.

"You're right, Gypsy, you shouldn't," said Connor, his voice quiet. "It's only a precaution, just in case."

I heard a buzzing noise—his telephone, which he reached inside his jacket to answer. "I'm sorry," he said, gazing at his phone.

There was a pause as he read the message and a look flickered across his face. I heard him swear quietly.

"I'm sorry, Gypsy, I have to go. I've tried to get in touch with someone key to the investigation and they've messaged me back."

Connor was already up and off the bed, and almost out of the room before I found my words.

"Connor, what's going on? Connor?"

But he was already gone.

*****

Connor bounded out of the ward, phone plastered to his ear. Finally, Aaron had sent a text and messaged him.

Pausing in a stairwell, he dialed the number. It rang twice.

"Connor?"

"Aaron, where are you?"

"On the move, listen…"

"Let me help, we can work this out together. Where are you?"

"Don't start with the usual cop bullshit, okay? Tiran's dead."

"What?" Connor stopped at the bottom of the stairs. "What are you talking about?"

"I went home to see Bailey. I found Tiran's body." His voice was ominously low. "I've done some bad shit, but I didn't kill her. I need *you* to find the bastard that did."

"Aaron, where are you? I can come and see you, we can work this out." Connor felt the vibration at the back of his throat, wondering if his voice had risen in pitch. He didn't want to sound too anxious, because it might scare Aaron off.

"We're past that, it's too late." Aaron's voice grew harder, his breathing noisy. "Look, I took Jo, she's with me, but I didn't kill her or Tiran. Jo had a report on her, a list of possible bent cops; I saw your name wasn't there. One of them probably paid Tiran a visit, though…"

"Aaron, let me help."

"Find the bastard that did this. I'm counting on you." The phone beeped in Connor's ear. Aaron had hung up.

"Damn." Connor jerked his head. He was outside the hospital. He picked up the phone again, dialing the number for Robson.

"Ian? Yeah, think we might have a homicide. Meet me at Aaron's place, I'll send through the address." Connor stalked off toward the car.

*****

Aaron was on his way back to the factory when he heard the news broadcast on the radio. The pigs had taken Jo. She was *his*, not theirs. He slammed on the brakes and howled with his mouth wide open, an animal guttural sound. He'd forgotten Bailey was in the car and now his son, distressed at the noise, was screaming at the top of his lungs. Shit. He pulled the van over to the shoulder of the road and flung himself out. He screamed again, wailing. It wasn't fair. It wasn't meant to be like this. They were meant to be a family. He picked up a large rock and threw it into a nearby field. When that didn't release his anger, he jumped, screamed, and kicked over a couple of fence posts. Bailey had gone quiet. He knew what he had to do. There were loose ends to tie up. He'd visit Stewart again. He had contacts and would help with the next step. Once he paid the stupid old bag a visit, he could move on.

He got back into the van and pulled a bottle out of the bag. Passing it over, Bailey took it and grabbed onto it like a lifeline, gripping it with his mouth and sucking on it hungrily. Taking a deep breath, Aaron started the car and pulled back into the main highway. He could be at Stewie's place in ten minutes.

*****

Connor pulled up to the front of Tiran and Aaron's home, hearing the tires on the gravel as he braked hard. His pace quickened as he headed for the boot to retrieve a pair of gloves and coverings for his shoes. In just a few strides, he reached the front patio, already snapping on his gloves. Stepping over the tape, Connor nodded at the constable guarding entrance to the property, taking the clipboard he held to sign in and headed up the porch stairs to step inside the front door. Ian Robson was standing by the body in the hallway.

Connor put the coverings on over his shoes to prevent crime scene contamination. The coroner's technician had arrived and was conducting a preliminary examination. Investigators were taking photographs and had begun marking off areas with tape, pacing as they marked each blocked off section.

"Ian, what's going on?" Connor knew he wasn't his usual self, struggling against giddiness. He'd known Tiran for a long time. This was the last outcome he'd imagined, never anticipating her murder, at that moment the numbness reassuring.

"Strangulation." Ian seemed distracted, pushing aside the tape and throwing his pen onto a side table.

"I talked to her not long ago and she was fine." Connor ran his fingers through his hair as he paced the small area.

"Bailey is gone. Aaron has him," Connor added, looking at Ian. "Tiran's partner. He called to tell me about Tiran. He found her body."

"You spoke to him?" Ian stood still, his voice steady.

"Yes, he asked me to investigate, said it wasn't

him."

Ian laughed roughly. "Oh well, case closed then."

The medical examiner spoke up, "No sign of forced entry."

"Holy shit," whispered Connor, the possibilities racing through his mind.

"So where's this nephew of yours, Connor? First that woman turns up almost dead in your warehouse, now his girlfriend winds up strangled, the baby nowhere to be seen," said Robbo, looking at Connor.

"I need to find him. I think it's time to pay one of his old dealers a visit. Stewart. If I know Aaron, he'll go there to work out what to do next." Connor placed a hand out beside him looking for a surface to lean on to combat the reeling.

"Well, what are we waiting for? The team has it under control. She's one of yours. We both know the care they'll take. Let's go."

Connor was surprised at his partner's all business approach. He hadn't known her but still…

"I can't leave now, she's family. I promised Aaron…"

He walked over to Tiran's lifeless body. Her open eyes were glassy, her protruding tongue swollen and purple. Her body was lying at a strange angle between the wall and the floor.

"I can't believe this. I talked to her yesterday. We thought Aaron would come home after he'd calmed down. Aaron doesn't have this in him. Kidnapping maybe, but murder, that's the last thing I expected."

"No one ever does, mate. People can always surprise us."

Connor approached the coroner's technician, Jacqui Gilbert. "I don't suppose you have an approximate time of death yet, Jacqui?" His chest was itching up again and he tried not to scratch it.

"Judging by the bruising on the neck and rigor mortis, I'd say tentatively sometime between 11 pm last night and 3 am this morning. I'll know more once I get her to the morgue. She put up a fight, though—we've found clothing fibers on the body and taken scrapings from under her nails."

"Thanks, Jacqui. Once you give me the all clear, I'll drop by."

"Let me guess, this one is a priority, right?" said Jacqui. As she leaned back on her heels, she wrote down notes on a clipboard.

"Yeah, if you could, I appreciate it. She was my nephew's de facto."

"Hmm, I heard. I'm sorry, Connor." She looked down as she eased Tiran's right limb gently to the ground.

"Well, Connor, I don't know about you, but I think it's about time we paid this dealer a visit," said Ian, adjusting his glasses.

"Like I said, Robbo, she's family. I can't just walk out of here."

"Don't you think the best thing you can do for her right now is find Aaron? I don't care what he says, this doesn't look good. The sooner we can find him the better."

"I don't know Ian…"

"Connor, let's go. You've been itching to find him for days. He's hiding somewhere and we need to find him before it's too late."

11

Leah arrived home from work haggard and worn out, her face grey and lined. Turning the key in the lock, she dropped the shopping bags on the table, and sank into a chair. They were really cranking up the pressure at work since they'd started making cuts.

Renee bounded in, with her smile lighting up the room.

"Mum, Mum! Guess what? Gyp says she's going to move in with us when she leaves the hospital! Isn't that great?" She was jumping up and down on the spot, her hands clasped together in delight.

"What are you talking about?"

"I talked to her today and warned her about the man. He's been looking for her. I told her it's not safe to go home, so she should stay with us for a while until things calm down." Two round rosy circles had formed on her cheeks.

"When did you go to the hospital? How did you get there?"

"Well…I, er… did that thing. You know that Gypsy and I do." Renee was shuffling her feet now and staring at the ground.

"Oh right, yes, that thing." Leah moved away and started packing food supplies into the refrigerator. She looked past her daughter to the cupboard behind.

"I'll have to think about this, Renee. It's been a long time since Gypsy and I lived together. I'm more worried about you at the moment. You know to wait at the school office and someone will escort you home, right?" Leah put the shopping away.

"Mum, *please*! It's important. She's not safe to go home. That bad man is looking for her!"

"Renee, I need to think about it. If you like, we can go in and see her again. I didn't think she'd be coming home so soon…"

"Okay, Mum, we'll go and see her again." Leah looked at her daughter as she left the room. Leah knew Renee would tell her to lighten up, but she had a bad feeling about this.

*****

Aaron pulled up outside Stewart's house. He grabbed the bag of nappies, bottles, and his son, Bailey, with his right hand. With the other hand, he grabbed the car seat and slammed the car door closed with one knee. Walking across to the gate, he jammed it open with his knee, swinging it open with a clang of metal. The knee-high grass was wet from the rain. At the top of the steps, he raised a fist to pound on the door.

The door swung open and Stewart's face appeared, his bloodshot eyes and mouth both gaping wide.

"Aaron, what the…" He had a few day's growth on his face, and his brown hair was standing on end at odd angles. The tracksuit had been changed and was no longer stained. Preparing himself, he cleared his throat, voice still hoarse and eyes red-rimmed.

"Is that how you talk to you best customers, Stewie?" At Aaron's menacing tone, Stewart took a step back, allowing Aaron entry into his home. The place had an air of neglect about it, and smelled like unwashed clothing combined with mildew.

"What's going on, mate?" said Stewart frowning.

"Something important," Aaron grunted. "Where's Karen? I need her to look after Bailey for a day or two."

"We're not really set up for babies, mate." Stewart scratched his groin, before sitting down in the dusty armchair. "Hang on a minute, Karen's out the back. Karen! *Karen!* In here, love."

Aaron came further into the lounge, shoving aside clothes piled up on a grotty looking armchair so he could sit down. Bailey wriggled on his lap.

Karen called out from the back of the house, "What's wrong?" The back screen door banged behind her as she came in. "I was just hanging out some washing."

Karen had dark stringy hair, with pale skin and dark circles under her eyes. She was so thin that her clothes hung off her. The smell of alcohol hung like a cloud as she padded further into the room.

"Oh, he's so cute! Can I hold him?"

Aaron handed Bailey over.

"Haven't seen you in a while," she said, hoisting Bailey onto one hip.

"No, I've got something important to sort out. I just need Bailey taken care of for a day or two. There are bottles, clothes and nappies in there." Aaron barely looked at Karen as he spoke, focusing his stare on Stewart. He needed results *now*.

"No problem, I'll be happy to take him. We'll have so much fun together, won't we, Bailey? I think I've got some cereal out back. He's probably hungry." Tickling Bailey's tummy, Karen headed toward the rear of the house.

As she left the room, Stewart shifted uncomfortably in his seat. "So what's this all about? I got you the license plates and now you show up with the baby, what's the go?" Stewart scratched the bristles on his chin.

"You remember that bloke you mentioned? The one that has connections and can get addresses and personal stuff? I need his help." Aaron rubbed his hands on his jeans.

"For who? What's going on?"

"I can't really say too much about it, but trust me, it's important. I need the address of Gypsy Shields, her phone numbers, the works."

"All right, I'll see what I can do, but it'll cost you."

"Stewie, I've done enough business with you that I reckon you can organize this favor for me." Aaron looked at Stewie with teeth clenched.

"Leave it with me."

"Get it soon. This one's urgent. Call me once you have what I need." Aaron slowly lifted his bulk from the chair. Stewart flinched slightly his head jerking back as Aaron headed for the door.

"Okay, mate, you got it. I'll be in touch soon."
*****

Connor and Ian pulled up at the curb in front of Stewart's house. Ian looked across at Connor, his hand perched over the lever ready to open the car door.

"You ready for this, mate?"

Connor had both hands on the steering wheel, and as he stared at them, he noticed his knuckles were white.

"Connor? You ready?" Ian's words jolted Connor out of his reverie and he dropped his hands from the steering wheel.

"Yeah, I'm ready." He opened the car door and got out.

The front yard was littered with rusted car parts,

knee-high weeds growing in between them.

Stewart's eyes rounded with surprise as he spotted Connor's badge. He didn't have any weed in the house that he remembered, but cops always made him nervous.

"Hello?" he said.

"Are you Stewart Johnson? I'm DC Reardon, and this is DC Robson," said Connor, flashing his badge quickly.

"What's this all about?" said Stewart, taking a small step backwards.

"We're here about a murder. A young woman—you might know her, Tiran Goldstein."

"Tiran's dead? What the…" Stewart shuffled back a step and his grip on the door tightened.

"We're hoping you can help us with our enquiries. We're looking for Aaron Reardon," said Ian, stepping forward. "Can we come in?"

"I'm sorry. I don't know anything about this." Stewart started to close the door, but Ian jammed a foot inside the doorway.

"Actually, we think you do," Ian said. "We know that you used to be Aaron's dealer, probably still are. He's gone missing. Has he been to see you recently?"

"Well…"

"Look, Stewart," Ian said, taking a step inside the doorway. "We can either do this here, or down at the station. Which would you prefer?"

Stewart relented and opened the door further. "Okay, I guess you'd better come in then."

Connor and Ian walked into the hallway, the unwashed smell wafting across to them. The lounge was littered with food wrappers and clothing. Connor and Ian sat on a ripped couch.

"Nice place you've got here," said Ian with a sneer.

Connor shot him a warning look.

"So, what can you tell us about Aaron? Has he visited you recently?" Connor pulled out a notepad and pen from his pocket.

"What happened to Tiran?" said Stewart, kicking some clothes out of the way, as he sat. The vinyl crackled as his weight hit the chair.

"She was murdered, strangled. Their son Bailey has disappeared. You wouldn't know anything about that, would you?" Connor leaned forward in the chair, one forearm across his right leg.

At that moment, a baby's cry echoed from the back of the house.

That sounded like Bailey. Surely, it wasn't though, he probably just imagined it. Had Aaron been here? He'd felt the creeping dread for days. He was certain Aaron wasn't the killer, but why the hell did he abduct Joanne Seyers? What was he thinking? And what would compel him to leave his son with a known drug dealer?

Connor's sympathy for his nephew was wearing thin. He didn't think this was the work of a disturbed young adult with a troubled past. It was the work of a tormented soul with evil intentions. He struggled to find the right words to explain it all.

Connor scratched his right cheek and stood up. He took a step toward the back of the house.

"You have children?" He took another step towards the source of the crying.

"Hang on a sec." Stewart stood up and followed him. "Karen? Are you there, love? The police are here," he called toward the back of the house.

Karen emerged carrying Bailey, smiling happily.

"What the hell is Bailey doing here, Stewart?" Connor's teeth were clenched.

"Er…well, Aaron came by earlier today. He needed a bit of a hand."

"I thought you didn't know anything about this," said Connor, taking a step closer to Stewart.

"Well, er, he looked pretty angry, and I figured it was best not to make things worse. He's got a temper on him. He said he had something important to sort out and he needed Bailey looked after for a while. He was in a bit of a hurry." Stewart was rubbing his hands through his hair as he paced.

Ian was poised and ready, one foot set in front of the other.

"What the hell did he want? Start talking. Now." Connor had taken a step closer to Stewart, and felt his nostrils flaring as he flexed his fingers.

"Look, it was said in confidence, okay?"

Connor launched himself at Stewart. He grabbed him by the top of his tracksuit and lifted him up against the wall.

"Listen, scumbag." He spat out the words, doing his best to control his fury. "One woman is dead and another one in critical condition. Aaron's son has suddenly turned up here, and you know nothing about it? Start talking or I swear…" Sprays of spittle landed on Stewart's jumper.

"He wanted the address of some woman. Said it was important. Some chick called Gypsy, he wanted her details."

Connor dropped Stewart and blew out a breath. Stewart fell in a heap, panting, hands splayed across the grimy carpet.

"DC Reardon, I think it's time for us to leave,"

said Ian rolling his shoulders. However, Connor's gaze remained fixed on Stewart. "So how are you getting this information to him?" Connors teeth were bared.

"I said I'd text or call when I have the info."

"Right. Well, give him that information and I'll see that you're charged with being an accessory to murder. Do we understand each other?"

"No problem. As soon as he calls, I'll let you know." Stewart was shaking now.

Connor threw his business card down at the man. "Let's go. Don't think you're keeping that child. His mother has been murdered, and he doesn't belong here. We'll be back for him, soon." With that, Connor stormed toward the front door. Bailey looked up at him blankly as he sucked harder on the pacifier in his mouth.

"Does he have any supplies?" asked Connor. Karen scurried away and returned quickly with the bag, which Connor threw onto the couch. Stewart ran to open the front door.

"We'll be back," warned Connor as he and Ian stepped back outside.

Ian turned to Connor before opening the car door. "So what they hell are you going to do with a baby? Where did you get that bright idea?"

"I can take him to Christie's place later if need be, I'll be damned if he's staying with a drug dealer. I'll talk to social services. We need to question her anyway. Get in," said Connor.

Connor's phone buzzed, interrupting the stillness. "It's the Coroner," said Connor, swiping the screen before holding the phone to his ear. "Jacqui? Any news?"

"That's why I'm calling. I heard this case was pretty close to you so I figured you could do with a favor. I thought you might like to go into the lab and take a look for yourself. Reece, one of my techs, has the details. He's expecting you."

"Thanks, I'll be there soon." Connor hung up and turned to Ian. "Change of plan. Jacqui has some test results, sounds like she's nailed the killer."

Ian turned his head quickly, his face going an unusual shade of grey. "Huh? What about the kid?"

"We can work that out later. I'll drop you back at the station."

"What? Hang on a second, Connor."

It was too late. Connor had already started the engine. Ian held on as Connor took off at speed, heading toward the central business district.

"What am I supposed to do, Connor? On your own now? Seriously?"

"I'll only be an hour or so."

"This is ridiculous." Ian shook his head.

"What do you want me to do? This is my fucking nephew, Ian. I need a couple of hours, alone."

Ian Robson didn't reply. They drove for a few more minutes, before Connor pulled up in front of the station.

Ian opened the door and got out. "The only reason I'm doing this is because it's family and I know you need time, mate. Let's get one thing straight, we're partners, okay?"

Connor took a deep breath. "Okay, mate, understood. I shouldn't be longer than an hour or two." As Ian slammed the door, Connor took off, heading toward the forensics lab on William Street.

Although Connor knew Aaron had gone into

hiding, he was certain his nephew wouldn't end another human life. Seeing the evidence would bring some closure.

The forensics lab was separate from both St Kilda headquarters and the Coroner's office, which Connor was thankful for. He'd unfortunately become familiar with the tiled walls and floors in the morgue, but he'd never quite grown accustomed to the decomp odors that the technicians didn't seem to notice, smells like sewage and rotting garbage combined with disinfectant. At least in the lab there would be no dead bodies or offensive stenches to distract him.

It was easy to find a parking place, and Connor entered the elevator, heading for the fourth floor of the building. He used his ID to grant him entry to the lab, the elevator doors giving way.

He walked onto the level, the hushed voices and the carpeted offices bearing signs to the laboratory. At the end of the corridor, a woman sitting at a desk looked up at him expectantly. He fished out his identification.

"Connor Reardon, Homicide. I'm here to see Reece, one of the technicians."

She gestured through the glass doors. "Go through, he's expecting you." She went back to reading her report and Connor headed in.

He saw a young man standing at a console perched on top of a very long white counter, and he made his way over.

"Reece?"

The dark-haired, cocoa-skinned young man looked up. "Detective Reardon? Jacqui mentioned you'd drop by. She fast tracked this one. Apparently, it's a fairly sensitive case…"

"Yes, thank you."

Reece clicked on the computer screen. "We've analyzed the scrapings from under the victim's nails, and compared them to a second sample we took from a hairbrush. Apparently, there was some suspicion that the killer was the victim's partner?"

"That's right," said Connor quietly, looking across at the display as he rubbed his chin. He saw multi-color images combined with technical jargon at the bottom of the screen.

"Well, as you can see here, the match is pretty conclusive. It's a 0.001% probability that her partner did this. The skin scrapings taken from under the victim's nails are not a match. We're still conducting further tests."

The gravity of the news hit Connor. He sagged against the bench and pressed palms to his eyes. He couldn't speak. His nephew was telling the truth.

"Detective Reardon?" The young lab technician said his name and he brought his head up out of his trance.

"Sorry, lost in thought. Can you say that again?"

Reece put down the report and turned to face Connor.

"Very low possibility that Tiran's partner murdered her. Not a match."

"Can you forward a report to me over at the station? I'm at Carlton."

"No problem, I'll fax it over just as soon as I can."

"You've been a great help. I appreciate this being rushed through."

"I'll let Jacqui know you were here."

"Thanks," said Connor, his mind racing ahead. He'd suspected for some time now that Aaron had been a party to the crimes, but now the killer was unknown, unnamed. Connor would need to begin the search again. Aaron was most definitely a kidnapper, but not a murderer.

"Please thank Jacqui for fast tracking this. I know how busy you guys are down here."

"Will do," said Reece, and Connor made his way back out of the building, heading back to the police station to collect Ian Robson and give him the news.

*****

12

Today the rehab room didn't feel quite so much like a torture chamber. Lyndall still stood at the end of the bars, smiling encouragingly, but my legs and arms didn't hurt like hell every time I moved them. In fact, I could pretty much work as I used to, other than the pathetic limp on my left foot. My speech was getting there too, so all was right with the world.

"You're making fantastic progress, Gypsy, well done!" Lyndall's brown hair flopped across her cheeks as she stood.

"I agree, definitely worthy of a reward of some description." I glared as I got to the end of the bars, and leaned against them with arms crossed.

"That's true. Sounds like you have something in mind." Lyndall was smiling at me.

"A discharge from the hospital soonish would do it. I could always come back for regular outpatient appointments." I looked at her, trying not to sound too hopeful.

"That's a point. You are making record progress. I'll need to talk to your care team, though. Would you like me to talk to your doctor and see what he thinks?" Lindy was rubbing her chin now.

"That would be great. I miss my flat something fierce. I've practically read every book available on the reading trolley. There's nothing quite like my own bed." I fussed with my shirt, pulling it down toward my hips.

"Okay, Gypsy, I get the point, I know you're miserable in here. I'll have a word with him and see what we can do. Although I'm a bit nervous about sending you home to your flat—you live on your own, don't you?"

"Yes, but my sister has agreed to have me stay with her for a while when I'm released…" Thank God, I think. I've got more chance of being sent home this way, thanks to Renee's suggestions.

"Great. Well, let's head back to your room, and I'll let you know how I get on with the care team." Lyndall headed toward the exit and I shuffled beside her.

As we headed toward my room, I realized that Renee and Leah were probably there waiting. My bond with my niece was getting stronger, thanks to her newly discovered abilities, which would definitely come in handy. Sure enough, as I squeaked open the door, there they were. However, this time, Leah had a genuine smile plastered across her face, a refreshing change.

She was sitting in the chair beside my bed, and her face looked bright. Considering this was the first time I'd seen her since we both said what we needed to, I was surprised. Interesting what a confrontation with your sister could achieve, I guess.

Renee rushed over. "Gyp! You're walking so well now, you look great!" Her eyes were shining, her cheeks rosy.

I ran my hand over her silky hair. "It's good to see you, Renee. I feel great." And I smiled, a real smile, feeling it broaden across my face.

"Gypsy." Leah stood up in front of me, light highlighting her blow-waved hair.

"Yeah, I feel pretty good, actually. My walking is getting better, and they're talking about sending me home soon. Bet you're excited about having me at your place." I couldn't resist.

Leah laughed. "Yeah, right. I want to keep my daughter happy. She's decided you're moving in with us. We'll see how long we last before killing each other, I guess." She looked at Renee, who had perched on my bed. As I sat down, she grabbed my walking stick, which she had taken a liking to.

"They might be discharging me in the next day or so, Leah." I studied her to judge her reaction.

"Tomorrow? Seriously?" Leah's smile had fallen from her face. "That soon?"

"Maybe, it depends on what the doctor says. I'll still need to come in for outpatient appointments, but yeah, they might send me home tomorrow."

Leah didn't seem quite so keen, given the rush, and the blood had drained from her face.

"Look, it's okay if you can't do it…" I extended a hand, wanting to give her an easy out.

"No, it's all right. I don't think it's safe for you to go home while this madman is still on the loose. I thought I had a bit more time to prepare, that's all. When will you know for sure?" I noticed the lines on her face.

"Later today, I guess."

"Just let us know as soon as you know. I was going to pick up a few of your things to make it more homely. Jerry says hello." A ghost of a smile appeared.

"Poor kitty, he must be lonely."

"Actually, he's been with us for days."

"He has?"

"Yes, he's settling in well. We couldn't leave your cat alone."

At this point, I'd just about had enough. I wanted to bask in the thought of going home soon, and I'd rather not have company. All I could think about was settling in for the night with that which was always comforting, the home shopping network. After suffering with insomnia for years, I had become addicted to it on late night TV. It wasn't something I liked to tell many people, but my cupboards were filled with exercise equipment, slicers, knife sets and juicers. It was where I felt most at ease. It was my zone. I knew the hospital phone wouldn't allow me to dial 1-800 numbers, but there was always the laptop, and I had my trusty credit card ready to go.

"Sorry, guys, don't mean to be rude, but I'm feeling a bit tired." I gave them my best tired, pitiful patient look.

"Oh, I understand, of course. We'll be back to take you home with us. Come on, Renee, let's go." Leah zipped up her handbag, hoisted it over her shoulder and headed over to pat my hand. Renee hugged me, gave me a look, and said, "See you soon, Gyp. I can't wait to bring you home."

The door closed behind them and I breathed a sigh of relief. I turned on the television, switched the channel to the home shopping network, fired up the laptop, and settled in for a relaxing night of shopping.
*****

Connor's niece, Christie, opened the door, her mouth forming an O in surprise.

"Uncle Connor? What's going on?" Her gaze moved to Ian Robson, and back to Connor.

"Sorry to just show up, but it's a bit of an emergency. Can we come in?" Connor had already turned his shoulder and was moving across the threshold.

"Of course." Christie opened the door wider and

stood back to allow them entry. "Can I get you a coffee?"

Connor stepped into the lounge, which was decked out with chrome and modern white leather furniture. "Coffee would be great. Strong, black, no sugar."

Ian followed Connor, taking a seat next to him. The leather couch made a rippling noise as he sat down, and he detected a smell of lilacs and roses coming from a large glass bowl of dried flowers on the shelf above the fireplace.

In the kitchen, cups readied, he heard the flick of a kettle switch and water slowly bubbling. Christie came back with coffee steaming in large black mugs, which she set on her black coffee table.

"Are you going to tell me what this is all about?" she said, her blonde curly locks falling forward as she leaned forward in the armchair.

Connor pulled at his earlobe. "It's about Aaron. I haven't been able to get in touch with him for nearly a week. There's been some bad news, I'm afraid."

Christie's fingers touched her parted lips and she gasped. "What sort of bad news?"

"Tiran was found murdered yesterday, and Bailey's been taken. We found him at Stewart's place—that's Aaron's old drug dealer; apparently Aaron was there earlier visiting him, asking for information."

Christie's face turned from slightly pink to a pale grey. "Tiran's been murdered? Oh, my God, I don't believe it, Bailey. It can't be true..." She covered her face with her hands.

"Christie, I know this is all very sudden, but I need to talk to you about Aaron's younger years. In particular, the bullying..." Connor looked at her intently.

"Well, that was a long time ago, Connor…"

"I know, Christie, but this is important. It may give me the answers I need. I need some idea where he's gone."

Christie set her mug on the coffee table, and rubbed her forehead with one hand, deep in thought. "Things were pretty rough there after Mum and Dad died, especially after the house burned down."

Ian looked across at Connor, adjusting his glasses.

"Christie, I understand it's difficult, but I need to know about the time Aaron tied you up. Can you tell us about it just once more? It's really important." Connor reached across to touch Christie's hand, and she looked up at him before letting out a sigh.

"That was years ago. You know what he's like. He always struggled with his temper." Despite her uncle's close proximity, Christie's gaze flitted from wall to wall and she blew out a few short breaths in an attempt to gain control. "That day, he was worse than usual. He'd been teasing me since the night before, telling me I was soft, and punching me in the arm, hard. I hadn't seen him that bad before. I raced home from school and locked him out of the house. He went berserk, screaming and beating on the windows and doors so loud I was worried about the neighbors reporting it, so I let him in. When he did get into the house, he scared me. He looked different, really mad, like crazy mad. He disappeared for a minute, and then came back with a length of twine." Christie paused for a moment.

"It's all right, go on," said Connor, leaning forward and urging her on with a nod of his head.

"Well, he grabbed me by the arm, hard. He pushed

me down onto a kitchen chair and tied me up. I cried and begged him not to, but it was like he wasn't there. He couldn't even hear me. When he had me tied up, he stood there yelling at me, how I was soft, how I needed to toughen up. That was when he pulled out a metal bar from the garage and threatened me with it. I didn't mention the bruises that formed on my arms the next morning where he hit me with the bar." She had her face in her hands now, shaking it from side to side.

"I had no idea about the metal bar," said Connor, his face changing color.

"I know. You were in the force, and I realized straight away that the metal bar made things more serious and I didn't want to get Aaron into trouble. He was all I had left." She pulled her hands away, the tears forming lines through her make up.

"What about the pets? Did you witness that?"

"No, I didn't see him do that. I would have tried to stop him. He knew how much I loved Blackie and Dolby. When I asked him what happened to them, he denied knowing anything. He said someone must have broken in. His story never rang true, but I knew better than to take him on about it." Christie paused.

"I thought we'd moved past all of this. It was years ago. Aaron met Tiran and got a job after Bailey was born. Made a fresh start." Christie took a deep breath.

"Tiran dead, it can't be, are you sure it was her?"

"I'm sorry, Christie, but we're sure. There's no doubt," said Connor. "I need to find him. Any idea where he'd go if he wanted to hide out?"

"Yeah, the factory in Laverton probably."

Ian looked at Connor and ran his hands quickly through his mop of jet black hair.

"Actually, we've already been there." Ian looked at the floor.

"You have? Was he there?"

"That's where Joanne Seyers was found."

"The abducted woman? Are you serious? Oh, my God." Christie's voice dropped to a whisper as the truth dawned on her. Then it rose to a high pitch as she screamed, "What the hell has he done? What the hell has my brother done?" She stood up and started pacing, shaking her hands in front of her.

Connor grabbed her by the wrists.

"Christie. Christie, look at me." She lifted her head and Connor spoke quietly. "It's going to be okay, I promise you. I'll find him. I promise."

Christie dropped her arms to her sides, and Connor eased her back down onto the chair.

"What about Bailey? What's going to happen to him?"

"I was hoping you would take him."

"Me? I work full time. There's no way I can look after a baby." Christie's face contorted.

"No, I meant you could take him over to Jill's place. We both know how she feels about kids, especially young ones. She'd love to have a baby in the house."

Christie dropped a hand from her hair to pinch her nose. "That's true. It would cheer her up having Bailey with her. Let me know." She raised shakily, Connor moving with her to touch her elbow to guide her to the kitchen.

"So what's the next step, then?"

"I'm not sure, Christie. All I know is I need to find Aaron soon. I'll let you know when I know more. We'll talk soon, okay?" Connor looked at Ian, giving him the silent signal that it was time to move on.

"Let's go. We've got this damn press conference, so we'd better put in an appearance," said Ian through thin lips.

Connor and Ian headed for the door, and Connor breathed deeply, preparing himself for the circus that was about to unfold at St Kilda Road Police Headquarters.

*****

I'd already started planning my escape. Lyndall had come back to report that the care team had decided that I could be discharged home, with frequent out-patient appointments. The news filled me with excitement. I'd see my cat, Jerry, and could settle myself into a normal routine again. My walking was improving, and was almost back to a regular gait, the walking stick only a formality. I no longer suffered from headaches, and my speech was almost back to its pre-injury state. Sure, sometimes it took me a couple of seconds to work out which word to use, but considering I'd almost been killed, I was pretty damn pleased with my progress.

The trick now was convincing the staff I'd be okay for release to my own home, without Leah. I wasn't worried. Surely, the force could arrange a police car or two to swing past occasionally. Meanwhile, I still had a police guard in front of my room, changing shifts regular as clockwork.

I wasn't stupid. I hadn't mentioned any of this to Leah, because she'd hit the roof. I did, however, understand the legalities of the situation. There was no legal reason for the staff to keep me within the hospital walls against my will. They simply couldn't do it. Of course, their perceived ethical and moral obligations over my care were a different story, but surely, I could find a way around that?

I'd always been a fast talker, and in this case, I'd need to use every ounce of persuasion. I'd already decided I didn't want to stay here for a minute longer than I had to. If they really pushed the point, I'd tell them that Leah would be visiting me at home on a regular basis.

I prepared myself for the battle ahead. I'd already started packing.

*****

After circling the car park three times, Connor finally found a space. He wasn't looking forward to the press conference, but he knew he had to get it out of the way. The cold drizzling rain didn't help his mood. He took the elevator to the foyer, and checked in with Bill at the front desk. Bill was a retired cop. His grey hair was cut short and he wore dark rimmed glasses. He smiled as Connor approached.

"Connor, long time, no see."

"Bill. Yeah, press conference. I can't say I'm looking forward to it." Connor reached into his inside jacket pocket, curling fingers around his badge.

"Third floor, they're just setting up. Good luck."

With a wave, Connor headed into the elevator.

The scene in the foyer of St Kilda headquarters was one of intense activity. Its white tiled floors and floor-to-ceiling windows gave the impression of a corporate head office, if it weren't for the armed guards parked by each of the four main entrances.

He joined the throng of people outside the elevator. The doors slid open and he headed in, wondering what was ahead. How would this go down? What did the media know, exactly?

Connor entered a large room, which was almost full. Directly ahead was a stage with a lectern. There were a couple of hundred seats that were almost filled. The wind was howling outside, until it seemed that the room was shaking slightly, and the rain was painting slash marks across the tinted windows. The lights offered a dim glow, except on the stage, where the chief was bathed in light. He stood to the right of the lectern, along with his assistant, Darcy Long, the Media rep, Jane Strickland, and Ian Robson. Shit, Connor was probably supposed to be up there, too. He realized he'd had an appointment in the chief's office before the press conference, which he'd conveniently forgotten about. He watched as the chief spotted him and whispered in Darcy's ear. Darcy looked over at Connor before heading down the stage stairs and heading toward him.

Connor recognized Kelly Lowden, one of the journalists in the crowd. Her head came up, and she smiled as she saw him. She stood up and sashayed over with a smile. Kelly was one of the few journalists he trusted. He'd worked with her during Project Beacon, and also slept with her twice after the split with his ex. Damn, she was probably going to ask why he didn't call.

"We meet again, Mr. Reardon. Although I have to admit I was hoping to hear from you sooner." Her perfume was sweet and heady, invading his nostrils. Kelly was just as gorgeous as ever, blonde, fit, tanned, with bright red lips, and huge green eyes. They'd gotten together a few months ago. Kelly was the main instigator, and who was he to argue?

The raw pain of his marriage breakdown had diminished, but it nibbled at him occasionally. He wondered about where it would all lead, usually at night as he stared into the inky darkness of his bedroom ceiling, seeking answers he now knew would never come.

He'd encountered Kelly during the Project Beacon investigation. Her smiles and ability to listen had flattered him, and while usually immune to casual banter, he'd agreed to a night out.

He remembered the way she had laughed with him over dinner, later taking his hand once they arrived back at his flat, guiding him to the bedroom, where she kissed him softly. He remembered the feel of her soft skin, her hair falling gently as she moved over him. Somehow, he hadn't called her after that, although technically there was no reason not to. She was stunning in every way. Despite sleeping together twice, at the time, he wasn't sure how to tell her she was a temporary fix to heal the gaping hole inside his chest since the split—someone warm and beautiful to share his bed, but he hadn't been ready to take it any further than that.

Connor ran his hand across his stubble. "Yeah, I know. I'm sorry, Kelly. I guess I just wasn't ready."

"Maybe you could make it up to me by telling me the real story behind this Seyers' case. Why was she found at your warehouse, Connor?" She gave him a steady look, her smile slow as she waited for his response.

"Come on, you know I can't talk about a current investigation." He was starting to sweat now, and could only hope she didn't notice.

"You know you can trust me, Connor. We've done

this before. Project Beacon, remember?" She flicked her hair and looked up at him.

"I remember, Kelly, I really do. I know I can trust you—if there's a story to be had, you'll get it. This one's different, though. Where there's family involved, things change."

"I know that, Connor. Let me in a little, though, okay?"

"Actually, you might not want to be seen with me. My career's on a one-way journey to the toilet." He nodded his chin toward Darcy Long, who had almost reached them, his face a steely mask.

Darcy stopped suddenly. At over six feet four, he towered over them, his bald head reflecting the light, the surly expression on his face commanding their attention and bringing the conversation to an abrupt close.

"D.C. Reardon, an urgent word, please. Excuse us, Ms. Lowden." Long's deep voice and serious look told them he meant business. Kelly reached into her pocket and retrieved her business card, passing it to Connor with a final look.

"It's okay. I know when I'm not wanted." She handed the card over. "Call me soon, okay?" With a waft of perfume, she was gone, her shapely legs carrying her quickly back to the press area.

Darcy Long was so close that Connor could smell his breath.

"Detective Reardon, I wonder if you fully grasp the seriousness of the situation."

Connor sighed, pulling at his earlobe. "Of course I do, I've been on the case for days."

"Really? The Chief was expecting you in his office an hour ago. He has news of vital importance that he needs to discuss with you…"

"Look, I got busy with the case, okay? I understand all of the implications, but…"

Darcy Long placed an arm on Connor's shoulder. "The Chief has asked me to escort you to the stage immediately."

Connor wrenched his shoulder away from Darcy, whose face was going red. "Get your damn hand off me."

The lumbering man took a step backwards, removing his hand. "Follow me."

"Listen, Darcy, I'll come with you, but there's not a chance in hell I'm getting up on that stage. Get me a seat in the front row, but the stage is not happening. You can jam it." Connor looked at him, his mouth set, the muscles in his cheek twitching as he fought for control.

"Wait here." Darcy Long clomped off toward the front row, with Connor following. Connor watched as Darcy leaned his long frame over to whisper in the ear of someone seated in the front row, who promptly rose and moved to sit in another chair. Just before the press conference began, Connor took his seat.

The Chief moved up to the lectern, and the click and flash of cameras began.

"Thank you everyone for your attendance today. As you know, Joanne Seyers, an employee of Victorian Police is recovering in the hospital. Her family is thankful for her recovery, and asks for privacy at this time. I can assure you that this active and ongoing investigation is receiving top priority, and a taskforce has been assigned where we are pursuing a number of enquiries…"

Connor had heard it all before, and the Chief's words merged into a hum of white noise. He noticed Kelly was staring at the Chief intently. After a while, her hand and a few others went up. It was obviously question time and Connor realized with a creeping sense of dread that bad news was coming.

"What can you tell us about the location in which Ms. Seyers was found? Rumor has it she was found in an abandoned factory owned by a senior detective. Can you confirm or deny?"

Connor froze, his attention now riveted on the chief.

Jack Reynolds cleared his throat, glancing down at his shoes before raising his head.

"Yes, I can confirm that Ms. Seyers was found at an abandoned warehouse. The property is owned by a member of Victoria Police. As I said earlier, the investigation is active and ongoing."

A murmur rippled through the audience, increasing in volume.

Another raised hand amongst the crowd was chosen from the rabble of voices, questions tumbling over one another.

The Chief gestured with a stiff nod. "Yes?"

"What can you tell us about reports that there was a recent murder involving the Reardon family, namely the death of Aaron Reardon's partner?"

The chief looked at Darcy Long before speaking. "That information is recent and we are unable to comment. We are still pursuing all possible avenues."

"Do you have any evidence linking this detective to the abduction?" The speaker was Kelly Lowden. Connor looked across at her, mouthing the words, "Thanks." She smiled thinly.

Jack Reynolds the police chief cleared his throat, hands clasped firmly on the lectern. "As I mentioned, this is a current investigation. However, I will say that due to ownership of the property, the member in question has been suspended from duties pending an investigation by our internal affairs team. Once he has been fully cleared, he will resume active duty."

Connor felt the blood rush to his face, his head pounding. He looked up at his partner, standing meekly on stage, but Ian wouldn't meet his gaze. Of all the traitorous, disloyal, media pleasing snakes, Jack Reynolds was King. Crimson rage blazed through him, as he fought to regain control of his emotions. So this was why the chief wanted to see him earlier. His chest was a locomotive, pounding madly, and he held firmly onto the seat, bending his head down, focusing on his knees.

"So you're saying Detective Reardon is a suspect? Surely without evidence that is purely a pre-emptive move?" called out one of the journalists, a tall man known as Tom Sheehan, high profile print reporter who also appeared regularly on a current affairs panel.

"I'm afraid that's all I can discuss. As I'm sure you understand, the investigation is ongoing. I'll hand questions over to our Media Liaison Officer. We will advise of any developments as they happen." He stepped from the lectern and stomped down the stairs toward Connor.

"You, me, my office, now," he growled as he walked past.

Connor's fists were clenched so hard he could feel fingernails biting into his palm. He propelled himself up from the chair, casting a look behind to see heads turned toward him, their faces suspicious. Kelly shot him a supportive smile, before he stomped after the chief.

13

I was feeling especially upbeat today, and had started packing my bag, smiling as I picked up a t-shirt, folded it, and packed it neatly in the bag. The doctors had been in to tell me I'd be going home—Renee and Leah could take me home later that day. Humming to myself, I folded a pair of purple pajamas, and I was stuffing them in the bag when the television in the background caught my attention. That sounded like Connor's name, didn't it? I wondered for a moment if I'd misheard.

"…in breaking news, a senior detective is currently suspended from duty, and being questioned in relation to his involvement in the Joanne Seyers' abduction case. Ms. Seyers was found at a warehouse owned by Detective Reardon's family in Laverton. He is being questioned further and has been removed from duty pending investigation outcomes. We'll update you on this breaking story as the situation unfolds…"

I covered my face with my hands. Within a second or two, I dropped them and I threw the clothing I had in my hands across the room and felt prickles under my eyes. Don't cry, dammit, don't cry. Ice moved through my veins, and I sank onto the bed. Could this be true? How well did I really know him? Is this why he didn't respond to my calls? Was he there at the factory with Joanne? My mind swam with the possibilities and I thought about the night we met, the night Joanne was attacked. Although it was only a few minutes between my departure from Sophia's restaurant, and stumbling across the kidnapping, it was enough time for Connor to leave the restaurant and commit the crime. Was Connor really the man who hurt me? Why? I felt nauseous and my head swam with possibilities. Could he have bolted from the restaurant to lie in wait for the young woman, Joanne? Surely, he wasn't that good an actor? I had been so positive that he was one of the good guys, exactly as he seemed, but my rock solid certainty had taken a blow.

I was attracted to this man, and had been positive he felt the same. I scanned through the pictures in my mind of that fateful night, searching for clues, some indication that he was not as he seemed. He was honest, handsome, charming, and hard working. What did I miss? Joanne was an employee of the police force, if anyone had wanted easy access to her it was possible Connor could have tracked her and ran from the restaurant to abduct her. Possible but probable? The doubt was churning and burning my chest.

I felt a chill along my back. Had I sent my niece into the lion's den? Was it Connor who attacked me Saturday night, and I'd led my niece right to him? Connor had found the victim, but how had he known she would be there?

I was devastated to have been so wrong about him, blinded by his looks and charm. Could I really have been so wrong about this?

My instincts were usually pretty good. Connor seemed to be a man of integrity. What were his motives? Why did he do this? Surely, this would ruin his career. My instincts had also told me that Connor was hiding something important. He'd closed himself off to me and now I needed him to spill the truth.

I headed over to the telephone and dialed his number. As expected, it went straight to voicemail. Next, I called Leah on her mobile. It rang only twice.

"Leah?"

"Gypsy. What's happening?" Leah sounded concerned.

"Have you heard the news?"

"No, I'm at work. What news?"

"It's Connor. He's being questioned about the abduction of Joanne Seyers. She was found at his property."

There was a pause.

"Oh, my God, are you okay?"

"No, of course I'm bloody not." I ran my fingers through my hair, which was quickly growing back. "I'm sorry, Leah." Another pause. "I really need to talk to him, but his phone is going straight to voicemail. What time do you think you'll be here to collect me for this fun-filled adventure we call sharing a place?"

"Funny, Gypsy." I heard Leah push out a long breath. "Glad to hear you're still a smart-ass. I'll be there straight after work, probably around six thirty."

"I'll see you then." As I pulled the phone away from my ear, I heard Leah's voice from the telephone handset calling me back.

"Gypsy, you still there?"

I pulled the phone back to my ear. "Yeah."

"Is that cop still posted outside your room?"

"What? Yeah."

"Good. I'll see you tonight." I heard the dial tone as she hung up.

I resumed packing my bag with more energy, stuffing clothes into the bag with greater force. If

Leah didn't get here in time, I would just head to plan B and discharge myself with a taxi to take me to the place I was longing for, home. The frustration was doing my head in, so much to do and so little time.

*****

Connor knew that if he had to look the chief in the eye seconds after his public humiliation he would do or say something he may regret later. What the hell—his career was over anyway, so what did he have to lose? He followed the chief down the corridor, which ran behind the press conference hall. Their shoes clomped as they came to an abrupt halt outside the elevator entrance that would take them to the fourth floor.

"You could have told me," hissed Connor once they were inside the grey steely box.

The chief's eyes were focused at an imaginary point on the door. "I would have if you'd turned up. A man is only as good as his word." His voice bounced off the elevator walls as the doors slowly closed.

"My word? Are you kidding me? What about respect? How's that for a word?" The elevator door opened and Connor strode ahead, overtaking the chief, fists swinging. Damn the man, he was a stickler for the book and for keeping up bloody appearances.

Connor pushed the door open hearing it knock against the doorstop before bouncing back an inch. He'd learned over the years to rein in his temper and let it simmer within. The pot was bubbling over, but he'd mastered the art of reining in the wild colt. Jack didn't need another excuse to denigrate him.

He paused near the doorway, his breathing heavy as he looked out of the window into the dark street below. He heard the sound of the rain washing against tires as automobiles hurried across the waterlogged road, ploughing their way home. He wished he was one of those drivers at that moment, travelling somewhere pleasurable, comparatively insignificant, to dinner at a restaurant maybe. Restaurants caused his mind to move to the night he met Gypsy, and he hoped she hadn't been paying attention to the news. His attention snapped back into the brightly lit room as the chief pushed roughly past him, knocking his body into a chair.

As Connor felt his shoulders sag, he raised his chin slightly and saw the plants on the filing cabinet behind the chief were brown and thirsty, dying a slow death. The dust on the bookshelves was thick. Piles of paper on the desk were so high they threatened to topple over.

"Your badge and weapon, Reardon." The chief's mouth was almost closed. He brought his purple-lidded eyes up from the piece of paper he had shuffled across the desk to glare at Connor. Connor felt a heaviness move through his gut, the doubt a morphing mass, before it settled to a stone.

"Seriously? Just like that? Hand over my badge and weapon? How many years have we worked together? You know how I operate. Doesn't that count for something?" Connor was doing his best not to sound hysterical, but it was proving more difficult than he thought. After all the years, the long hours, time away from his family, the breakup of his marriage, had it really come to this? His case close rate was legendary, and here the chief was asking for his badge and weapon out of fear of public opinion?

"Don't make this any more difficult than it should be." The chief shook his head, his expression somber, and his chin moving closer toward the desk.

"You make my public suspension sound like a formality, a procedure. This is my life we're talking about. No one is more committed than I am." Connor's arm swept across his body in a sweeping gesture, his palm turned in a slicing motion. Over the last ten years there hadn't been a single officer disavowed during a press conference. Whatever the hell the chief's hidden agenda, he needed to dig it out, and fast. "Any idea how the media scrum out there knew about the investigation?"

What Jack wouldn't say was a chain around his neck weighing him down. For him to come out like that and publicly suspend him was an aberration, bizarre beyond belief. Jack was saving face, but for why or for who was yet to be determined. There was no way he was going to make this easy, not a chance in hell. Connor crossed his arms, leaning back in the chair.

"You heard them." Jack Reynolds pointed a finger at the wall. "Joanne Seyers was found at your property. You must know how this looks."

"My investigation and suspension is a damn formality, we both know that. A farce to keep the papers happy. We heard them say they know that Tiran was killed by my nephew. I'm pretty sure DNA will prove that he didn't. How does that look? Is that really what this is all about? Perception? PR? For real, Jack?"

Connor's eye was drawn to the chief's throat, where the Adam's apple bobbed as Jack swallowed.

Snatched by a rush of resentment, Connor held up a palm partially obscuring Jack's face. "Let me guess the strategy here is to take any possible power out of negative press. A disgraced detective. The only flaw in that plan is that other than a piece of paper, you have nothing on me, not a shred of damn evidence! To hell with the team, the force itself, all that matters is how it looks to the blokes holding mikes. The least you could do was call me before the press conference. Isn't that what phones are for, Jack?"

His career was over, Connor had tried to control his anger, but it had all come rushing out. The years of frustration, the late hours on the job with little to no acknowledgment. Most cops didn't do it for a well-timed pat on the back, but when faced with uncompromising disloyalty, he'd cracked, his anger pushing him over the brink into a confrontation he'd been resisting for years. He'd pissed Jack off and his career was in tatters.

Jack sagged back in his chair. "Listen, I don't like this any more than you do, Reardon, but think about the implications. Until this is over, I want the force's reputation intact. I've moved to damage control. As soon as the evidence is in, you'll be reinstated. We both know this is only a formality."

A formality?

Connor wasn't capable of pushing the argument. His bones were aching and his hands trembling. Better just to hand it all over.

He reached into his jacket and felt the cold solidity of his weapon. It had been his constant companion. It had shot a man dead. He wrapped his fingers around the handle and withdrew it, dropping it onto the desk with a clatter. Jack held his head in his hands.

Connor reached into his back pocket to slide out his badge and grimaced, the heat behind his eyelids searing as it built to an ache. At that moment, he realized it was over. This was the end.

"Nothing can make this any worse than it damn well is," said Connor, his deep voice rippling through the small office.

The veins in the chief's cheeks were red. He ripped off his hat, throwing it at the cupboard in the far corner of the room.

"We're here to make damn sure law-abiding citizens are free to live without danger, but not at any cost, Reardon. It's time to give up for a while, a few days. It's over. Take some time out. We'll talk next week."

"That statement's true. That's something, I guess. We're a team, except your team includes politicians, journalists and internal affairs, which I want no part of. Let me guess, they're here already, right?"

The chief shuffled a piece of paper on his desk. "Right down the corridor. They'll cover the few questions that need to be asked. Starting with where the hell you were on the night Joanne Seyers was abducted."

"Bite Me? Great," muttered Connor.

"Excuse me?" said the chief, his head jolted up.

"Bite Me. Bittern and Meagher, you know the pride of the force."

Jack glared at him.

"Oh, you weren't aware of their pet names," said Connor. "What the hell, in for a penny…" He started to move out of the chair.

The chief shuffled his papers awkwardly, clearing his throat. "Well, that's it for now. I had hoped this could be quick and painless."

"Perfect, just fucking perfect," Connor whispered. The pain in his back surged upward as he stood. He turned to go, and leaned over to the chief.

"Hope you sleep well tonight."
*****

My bags were packed neatly and waiting patiently beside the bed. There were only so many times they could be packed and repacked. I decided to pass the time by flipping magazines, staring out the window, or walking around the ward, but after what seemed like many hours, it had lost its appeal. Surely, this was straightforward. They couldn't keep me here without my consent, could they? I walked out of my room yet again, and stood in the doorway, arms folded, tapping my foot, waiting until I caught someone's eye.

"Yes, Gypsy, the doctor knows you're waiting. He won't be too long."

I glanced across at the police officer posted outside my room—a different one today, curly and red-haired—and caught the eye of a nurse at the station. I couldn't give them too much of a hard time. They held my fate in their hands, but I figured a bit of badgering of a young greenish looking policeman could help pass the time.

"Lucky you, you get to knock off early today. No more standing outside the grumpy woman's room." I saw the ghost of a smile slide across the officer's face as he looked at me through the corner of his eye. "It's okay, I won't bite," I said. "I've asked for an early discharge. They're just working it all out now." The silence was deafening. Okay then, back to my room.

I closed the door loudly and resumed my position on the bed, flipping on the idiot box. I wished someone would hurry up or I'd end up calling a taxi and to hell with the consequences.

The daytime soapies were playing and I let out a sigh. Surely, television executives didn't imagine we were that desperate for entertainment. Like most of them, this one could be watched once a quarter whether I wanted to or not; so mind-numbly repetitive that I could miss three months of it, come back and take up where I left off.

I thought I heard the self-important tones of what was probably a doctor outside my room.

"This one here, this is Ms. Shield's room? She's ready?"

Yes, I am, I've been waiting here for ages, growing cobwebs, just damn well send me home!

The door opened and a man in a grey suit walked in. He looked to be in his late fifties, his grey hair freshly combed and wet. He flicked a look at me as he stood at the bottom of my bed.

"Ms. Shields," he said, raising an eyebrow, "I've been told you're eager to go home."

"That's right," I said, one arm set across my chest. "There's absolutely no reason to keep me here. I can walk unaided, my speech is fine, my rehab is done, I think. The best thing for me now is the comfort of home."

"Well, that's strictly a matter of opinion." The doctor didn't sound convinced. "I've been advised that you were the witness to a crime, which of course is the reason for the police guard. Are you really sure you want to go home at a time like this? The care team is concerned about your well-being, and we aren't convinced going home is the best idea at this time."

Great. I folded my arms. I felt like pacing around the damn room, but knew it wouldn't help my case. "I'm a grown woman, and the police escort, well, that was arranged without my knowledge. I'm been told by a senior detective that there will be police cars driving past my premises, and that's apart from the fact that my sister has said she'll be collecting me. She finishes work around 5.30 tonight, so we're really only talking about a matter of hours on my own…"

Mr. Grey-Suited doctor thrust his hands into his pockets. "Ms. Shields, I'm still not a hundred per cent convinced. If anything untoward happens…"

"But nothing will happen. Fort Knox is protecting me, for God's sake." I rubbed my brow hopefully to shove away the beginnings of another headache. "So you're telling me that you are going to keep me here? Whoever did this has no idea where I live, and in the time it takes to find me, my sister will be there to pick me up. The odds of someone tracking me down over a couple of hours are so small. I'll be fine. I understand the need to be safe, but I'm going stir crazy in here."

The doctor rubbed a hand over his chin as he frowned, and jammed a hand into his trouser pocket. "Maybe. You really are miserable in here, aren't you?"

An indefinite pause.

"Leave it with me. I'll need you to sign some paperwork, though…"

Yes!

"Of course, not a problem, I'm happy to sign whatever you need." I didn't want to let on that my heart had started pounding like a mad dog, didn't want to scare them in my moment of triumph. "My sister Leah, will be here soon, like I said, so it won't be a problem." I tried my best not to squeal and dance. I wanted to skip and jump—hell yes, I was going home!

*****

Connor was standing in the corridor outside the chief's office when his pocket buzzed with a text message from Ian Robson. *Sorry, mate, I honestly had no idea.* Ian probably wanted to mumble how sorry he was and hang his head, but knowing the pressure forced onto him, Connor guessed his partner would have reached the press conference early, and after a browbeating from Darcy, the pressure too much to bear, and paralysis enforced his inaction. He scowled down at his phone, an index finger hovering over it ready to reply when a man dressed in a brown suit from the seventies walked toward him.

"D.C Reardon? A word, please."

Oh great, it was Bittern, the Bite in Bite Me. Both Bittern and Meagher, the internal affairs reps were the butt of countless jokes, not only because of their dress sense, but because of the countless arrogant assumptions made by the only IA rep an officer usually had the displeasure of meeting. Officers talked at barbeques, usually right before Connor turned away to tune out of the conversation. He'd rather be alone than join in with the beer binges shared by some officers. He knew it was a one way ticket to tragedy.

"Not a good time, I have a victim to protect. She's the only witness to the Seyers' case, and if I don't move soon, I'm concerned she'll do a runner and discharge herself." He now knew the prickles and pinging was Gypsy, doing her best to get in contact with him with limited success.

Bittern shoved his hands into his pockets. The

lights shone on his almost baldhead. He'd spread the remaining threads of hair across it and his grey tie was loosened.

"I understand you're busy, Detective Reardon, but this will only take a minute. This way…" Bittern gestured with an outstretched hand toward the conference room door. Connor resigned himself to at least ten minutes with a couple of half-wits.

The door creaked, as it swung open. There was Meagher in a grey suit matching Bittern's. His handlebar moustache and haircut meant Connor bowed his head slightly to hide a half-smile as he reached the boardroom table. Meagher extended his hand to shake Connor's.

"I'd rather not," Connor said, thrusting his hands into his pockets.

Meagher fell back into the seat at the long polished table, clasping his hands together. Connor wondered if this was an attempt to appear efficient, all show, and no damn substance.

"Look, I don't have long," said Connor, looking at Bittern and then back to Meagher. "As far as I'm concerned, this is no longer needed."

"Look, Reardon, we understand we're not the force favorites, but there are some questions."

"You went to the press conference? My suspension is a joke."

"What does that mean?"

"The whole bloody country knew about my suspension before I did."

Bittern spoke first. "Well, ah, that's not strictly in our control. Those decisions are made by the chief or commander."

"I know, but after twelve years of service, who

would have thought? You probably got a kick out of it. Did you, Meagher?" Connor pushed himself back in his chair, resting his legs on the table supports underneath.

Meagher cleared his throat, looking down at the table's wood finish. "That's not for me to comment on. What I would like to talk about is the property in Laverton registered in your father's name."

Connor realized the reason for the hand clasping and paper shuffling. Bite Me had a copy of the property title on the table. Smarmy little pricks, they wanted him to see it.

"I see you have the deed to our warehouse there."

"Just some due diligence," Bittern said, eyes pinched.

"Due diligence? Is that what you call it?" Connor let out a snort. "Is that like the due diligence before I was publicly suspended?"

Bittern pushed his elbow further across the table, leaning so hard on it that it slid across the table clumsily. "Look, Reardon, like I said, we're here to ask questions, nothing more. The sooner we get answers, the sooner we're all out of here."

"It's public record now. I had an instinct and needed to check it out. I was as shocked as Ian Robson to find the victim there…"

"What prompted your decision?"

"To visit the warehouse? Partial registration details of a van."

"That's it?"

"Well, a few things, when you consider them individually didn't mean much, but in light of the witness account and the partial plate…"

"I see," said Meagher. "Our concern is your

knowledge of your nephew's involvement in this."

Connor pushed his chair across the carpet "Right, well, I need to check on this witness."

"The interview isn't over."

He sat back down, strumming his fingers on the table.

"There's still the matter of the deleted report."

Oh, shit.

The room swung into sharper focus. Connor knew Meagher was referring to the report that had been edited while Robbo was in his ear at the station last week. He'd processed it, and then as an afterthought, shifted its status to 'pending,' effectively moving it out of the active system.

"That was an afterthought. I was concerned about witness safety."

"Why would the witness be in danger?"

"Look, it wasn't strictly speaking deleting a report. It was moved from active status to pending."

"Go on," said Bittern, perched on the edge of his seat. He didn't move an inch as he waited for Connor's reply.

"It was a precaution. There were a few possibilities at the time and additional risks. I wasn't convinced Aaron was the perpetrator. There could have been additional suspects."

"Possibilities such as?"

"Given the sensitive nature of the report that Ms. Seyers removed, it's possible a corrupt member of police had targeted her. My goal was purely and only to get evidence. I wasn't sure a family member was involved. Who would be?"

"You weren't sure if your nephew was directly involved? Well, he was." Meagher's moustache twitched and he lifted up his chin to adjust his tie.

The chair almost fell over as Connor stood up, feeling for the keys in his pocket.

"I'm done. This interview is over." His voice shook slightly as he headed for the door.

Bittern stood up, his hands up in supplication as he moved closer to Connor.

"Try to calm down…"

"Calm down? This is my fucking career! I've sweated bullets, spent time away from my wife, my family, so don't tell me to calm the fuck down." Connor's face was moist, early glitters of sweat on his forehead, his teeth clenched, his long brown finger inches away from Bittern's face.

"Just a few more questions…"

"Move away from me, Bittern, now. This is it." Struggling to control his temper, Connor scraped the chair away from him. "What about integrity? Trust? I've been in the force twelve years, not a ripple, not a blemish and suddenly you want to crucify me, for what? Fucking appearances? None of you has mentioned the contributions I've made, the sacrifices. Here I am, slammed over a barrel because of an abduction and murder I wish my damn nephew had no fucking part in!" Connor's shoulders were like pistons, but his hands had fallen to his side. He looked around, realizing where he was, and sunk back into the leather chair.

14

Renee opened the door with a creak to see Paul, her father, filling the doorway.

"Dad!" she rushed into his arms.

"Mum home?"

"Yep, Mum's home, she's getting ready. We're picking up Gypsy from the hospital in half an hour and now you're here. It's so exciting!" Renee skipped along the tiles, leading Paul by the hand to the kitchen, where Leah was rummaging through her handbag.

She looked up, her mouth open. "Again?"

"What do you mean, again?"

"You, turning up out of the blue."

"How is this out of the blue?"

"No warning, no idea you'd be here. I need some notice, Paul."

"Why?

"Because of what you did! Don't you see, every time you roll up you might as well just stab me." Leah turned away, head slumped.

Paul followed her, raising his hand to touch her shoulder before realizing the folly of the gesture. "I guess I'm not sure if you'll see me. Surely, we can talk, try again?"

Leah turned to face him. "That's a big thing to ask, Paul. Even someone as dumb as you knows that."

"Guess so."

The silence between them was long and aching, heavy with unspoken words.

"So what are you saying?"

"I want to try."

"You did try, Paul, and you failed, pathetically and

miserably."

"Name the time and I'll be there."

"Jeez, Paul, I wasn't expecting this." Leah ran her fingers through her hair, oblivious to Renee around the corner. Renee was lurking in the hallway, crossing her fingers, her arms, everything she could think of if it meant Mum and Dad would get back together. She'd give just about anything to have them back together again.

"So why are you talking to me, then? Rita lost interest, did she?"

Renee wished her mum would shut up. If she kept on like this, Dad would never want her back.

"It didn't work out. It was just a flirtation, a fling. Nothing happened."

"But something did happen! It's called betrayal, Paul. How do you think I felt when I read your sexting messages with some random bitch from work?"

He paused the way he did when he wasn't sure what to say next. "I don't know. I suppose it's taken time for me to realize what an idiot I was."

"Past tense?"

"Okay, can be. She doesn't get me the way you do. After everything, all the years together, the ups and downs, it's us I want, Leah."

"So you don't want her then?"

Leah looked at him, waiting for an answer to something that had been a fleeting thought in the chaos that was her daily struggle lately.

"No," he said, "there's only one woman for me. Always has been."

"I'll think about the counselling that you refused weeks, no, months ago. What happens to this bloody harlot, this Rita work slut, then?"

"Don't call her that."

"Well, what should I call her then, your fucking mistress?"

Leah hadn't wanted to use the m word. Somehow, this was something that happened to other families, not them. Even their friends had told Paul he had the perfect life, the perfect wife. So what the hell went wrong? Sure, she took him for granted a little, but most married people did, didn't they? They were a couple, a unit, or she thought they were.

This was different. This was another woman, even if it was only dirty phone messages.

"Talk to me in a few days, Paul. No promises, but I'll see."

His shoulders dropped. "You won't regret this. We can make this work. I know we can."

"Don't make promises you can't keep. This was always going to be a shit storm."

"Less rough than splitting, Leah. Look, I'm not asking to move back in—I'm in a hotel until things settle a bit—I'm asking for a chance."

"You've had chances, Paul. Sometimes a marriage crumbles because of little things. The times I cried myself to sleep, all the small misunderstandings, the annoyances, they build up over time. I'll have to think about another chance."

Paul turned away from her and shuffled his feet.

"Let me know when you've thought it through," he said. "You know where I am."

*****

Renee's new ability, sprung from the necessity of being unable to reach me physically had planted the seed of an idea. If she could track me down and establish communication from a distance without being in physical contact, could I track this evil fucker down and find out what he was up to? It was definitely worth a try. If she could try out new abilities, I sure as hell could.

I thought about the night my life changed and I was left for dead in a dirty smelly alley. Surely, I could find him by revisiting the scene. With my intuition, once I was in the bastard's space, I was confident I could pick up on his signature.

I focused, seeing the journey from the air. I found the laneway, which looked vastly different during the day.   Litter blew along it, and it looked less malevolent, the stark reality of daylight slightly different to my memories of that fateful night. Although, of course, the van was gone, his stinking presence remained. I knew that degree of bitter twisted energy hadn't left, it lingered like an unseen mist, a gas that poisoned the minds of those around the source.

As I scouted the scene, the hairs on the back of my neck and arms prickled on end. We were getting close. I felt a pinging, a crack in the universe opening up. A mist rushed at me before a new scene appeared complete with the smell of unwashed clothes and mildew.

Did he know I was tracing him? In the small dank apartment, he looked over his shoulder.

The hunted was now the hunter.

At first, I saw the edges, the periphery just the couch and chair. Slowly but surely, like paint stripper across a dormant secret, I saw it. There they were, two degraded souls planning and talking, holed up in a neglected flat, dirty unkempt and malevolent.

Holy fucking shit.
It was Aaron, you sly little fucker.
My potty mouth had been unleashed.

Connor's secret silent burden at last made sense. On the night we met, Aaron had time to grab Joanne, and had to be the reason his uncle was keeping secrets from me. I felt relief that the pieces had slotted into place, tinged with guilt at ever doubting Connor. I remembered the nagging doubt I felt on the night I met him, an instinct that he was not as he seemed.

There was a damn understatement.

As I listened to the depraved creatures' conversation, my sly grin grew wider, allowing my vengeful plans free rein to fester and simmer.

So you planned on breaking in and scaring the shit out of me, did you weasel? Bet you didn't count on me being telepathic, you little shit.

Right now, I needed Renee to put my rapidly forming plan into action. Plus before my discharge, I needed to find and raid some hospital stash.

*****

Renee was curled up in bed with a book relaxing. With everything that had happened, she needed to switch off, and go to a world where misery and injury weren't the main features.

Chapter three was looking pretty good when she felt a pinging, a knocking on her soul, by someone seeking entry.

Gypsy, is that you?

This was becoming a habit.

The connection was a hook taking hold, the line cemented.

She not only heard the voice reverberating through

her head, but she saw her aunt in the hospital room.

It's urgent. I need you. How soon can you get here?

Gypsy looked back to her normal enthusiastic kick ass self. Today she was glowing, eyes bright. Renee saw Gypsy's tongue dart from her mouth to wet her lips. She certainly had something to look forward to. Probably going home had perked her up. If Gypsy was so excited though, why was she pacing and biting her lip?

Renee, I need your help. It's a lot to ask but you're almost as much in this as I am.

Renee fiddled with the book to keep her hands busy.

What do you mean? What's going on?

Whatever this was, it seemed to have brought Gypsy back to life.

I've got a plan to take that bastard down. I found him, tracked him. He's made it clear what he plans to do with me.

Renee scratched her forearm, and moved an arm to her stomach, which was gurgling and swirling. This was way out of her league. Her aunt's new attitude of action taking was a positive step, but not at any cost. This meant she'd been right when she sensed the creep a couple of days ago. The horrible man really was hunting her aunt and tracking her down.

He could hurt or even kill you. I don't think this is a good idea, Gypsy.

Relax, honey, I've got it all figured out. Your dad will help you, especially when you tell him about the slime ball trying to abduct you.

Renee sat up with a jerk, the book falling to her side. Her pulse quickened and she took a deep breath. She wondered if she could do this, if she had it in her to carry through with Gypsy's plan.

I'm not sure I can do this, seriously.

What's the alternative? That he waits for me in my bedroom, ties me up and tortures me slowly? I'd rather not find out what torture feels like, Renee.

Gypsy sounded anxious for the first time she could remember. Renee lifted a hand to bite a nail. As Gypsy showed her pictures of what he had planned, the horror crept up her back, tickling her spine and her muscles went on high alert, rigid and tight. She remembered the day the man had followed her home from school, the fear a tightly packed ball in her stomach, the ringing in her ears, the overwhelming relief washing over her when she reached the safety of home.

She had the chance to stop him from hurting her aunt. She felt the ball in her stomach melt away under a slow burn. She wrung her hands. Her eye caught the glint of her bracelet that she twisted around her wrist. The noise of her breathing reached her ears.

Do you really think we can do this? Can we stop him?

She saw her aunt stand up, hands on her hips.

We can do more than that. We can make him pay. Tell Paul you need to come to the hospital urgently. It's an emergency. Don't tell him any more than that. I'll do the explaining. Most of what we need, you'll find in the hallway cupboard at my place. Some of it Paul will need to find. Mark left some of his hunting gear behind. We can put it to good use.

*****

Aaron's leg muscles were tight. He was sitting in the car but ready for action. The day before, Stewie had come through. Although the bitch was dumb enough to have her address on her business website, Stewie had agreed to case the place with him. At two in the morning, they'd taken a walk around and checked her place out. The bathroom window on the far corner was dark enough and would provide the easiest entrance for a break in. They'd tried it and the window wasn't locked.

The windscreen had misted up. He grabbed an old rag from the floor of the passenger seat and wiped it with a squeak. For days, he'd been looking forward to tonight. She was the reason he'd failed. She was the reason Tiran was dead, this stupid Gypsy bitch. Now she would pay. He wanted to hurt her, watch her squirm, witness the suffering and pain move across her face, to smell the sweat and the fear oozing from her pores.

Stupid cow, he hadn't needed the address from Stewie. The ugly whore had her address plastered all over the internet for anyone to see. He found her website, "Business Words," and there she was on the contact page. It had been an unexpected gift.

He fingered the handle on the bag behind him. His crowbar was in there, sitting on the top of a pile of tools for easy access. Through the cleared section of windscreen, he could see the trees, their branches barren and brittle, the leaves piled along their base. The grey concrete was a line of steel, and ice seemed to hang in the air. He shifted uncomfortably in his seat. He'd just about had enough. It was a go, now. He got out of the car and turned the key to lock it.

The noise of a truck rolling down a hill snapped him back to the present.

He thought about this old bag, and about how her walk in that damn alleyway had wrecked everything. She had no reason to head into a black laneway. Why the fuck was she there? He thought about Connor. Now there was the perfect example of hypocrisy that he'd lived with for years. The big shot police detective, taking in two orphan children, couldn't have children of his own. He no longer believed he and Christie were brought into his home for love; more for convenience than anything.

He knew the reality.

His sister was actually his cousin. Connor was her father. It wasn't hard to work out, any fool could see just by looking at them. Yet, Aaron had paid the price. He'd suffered the shame and pain of his parent's constant preference for his sister. Then he'd lost his dad, followed by a pathetic excuse for a mother, and then an uncle that couldn't keep his pants on became his adoptive father. Connor had always favored his sister. It was obvious. He'd tried not to let the wounds fester and turn gangrenous, but it wasn't easy watching the way Connor treated Christie—the smiles, the shining eyes, the abundant affection. Christie got the attention, the best schools, and the beams of pride. They'd never expected more of Aaron, so he hadn't bothered. He'd hassled Christie about it a bit, but nothing she didn't deserve. What, did they think he was brainless?

He'd known it would come to a head one day, and here it was. He hadn't planned on grabbing Jo Seyers, the impulse had rolled across him in a wave of attraction and lust, turning his legs weak and his head giddy. There was something about the moment, their fate, both of them together for eternity, forever.

He thought he'd loved Tiran, but it wasn't until he saw Jo that he realized she was the one, the soul mate, a woman he was meant to be with forever. It had escalated from there. Tiran didn't understand him, didn't try hard enough, was too wrapped up in the baby and ignored him, resented him. At first, he thought he'd just talk to Jo, maybe get her number, take it slow, but when she swore and then laughed at him, it had tipped him over the edge and he'd grabbed her.

He was still coming to grips with losing both of them. Opportunities were for the taking. He needed to make it right, and making Gypsy suffer would cancel his misery out forever.

Gypsy Shields could be silenced permanently. He'd sort his uncle out later. He could feel the anticipation coursing through him, and his limbs twitched with excitement.

A couple of hours, then it would all be over. Justice would be his.

*****

Leah looked completely shocked, flabbergasted in fact, her mouth open, her eyes wide. She was leaning over the counter of the nurse's station.

"She's what?"

"Ms. Shields discharged herself a couple of hours ago."

Leah went pale. Pursing her lips, she turned away from the desk slightly in an effort to control herself. Failing miserably, she slapped her hand down on the bench around the nurse's station. There was a sudden silence; heads turned.

"What do you mean, discharged already? She had a bloody police detail outside her room!" Leah let out a sigh as she waved her hand. "I don't believe this," she muttered.

A blonde nurse eyed her off. "I can understand you're upset, but there was nothing we could do to keep her here. We did try to persuade her. She was very insistent, and told us she would be staying with you. She'll be back in a couple of days for her outpatient appointments."

Renee peered up at her mother, placing a hand on her waist for comfort.

"What's going on, Mum? Where's Gyp?" Renee was frowning and staring at the nurse, hoping for an answer.

"Not now, Renee, seriously. Why the hell they discharged her early, I will never know." Renee shook her head as she moved away from the nurse's station. When she was a few meters away, she called, "Let's just hope nothing happens to her, otherwise it will be on their heads. There wasn't a policeman parked outside her room for the fun of it. You would think they would know that."

"Mum, calm down. Let's go." Renee was starting to feel embarrassed. She had a feeling Mum was going off on one of her tirades.

Leah headed off, her steps quickening as the gravity of the situation dawned on her with each step.

"Let's go, hon. We'd better make sure my bloody sister's all right."

15

Connor had been ringing the number for Gypsy's phone beside her hospital bed, but it was ringing out, time after time, the tone pulsing in his ear. He decided to ring reception. Maybe the nurses in the ward would know what was going on.

"Hello, St. Vincent's Hospital."

"Yes, hello, Detective Constable Reardon here. I'm looking for Gypsy Shields in Ward 3B. Can you put me through to the nurse's station, please?"

"Certainly."

The line clicked as the receptionist tried transferring his call. If he got put through to the wrong department, he'd probably end up kicking the nearest inanimate object. He'd had enough.

"Hello, 3B." The woman's words came out so quickly and were so garbled that Connor had no idea what she said.

"Yes, hello, what ward is that?"

"3B." The nurse's voice had an edge of barely contained impatience.

"Oh, good, I'm looking for Gypsy Shields. I've been ringing the phone in her room and it just rings out."

"One moment, please." He heard keys clicking in the background. The nurse must have been looking her name up on the computer.

"Let's see, Gypsy Shields. Yes, here we go. She was discharged earlier today around four thirty."

Shit, she was already gone.

"Can I ask, did she go home with her sister? There is a potential security issue with this patient. She was the witness to a crime. You noticed the police guard outside her room?"

"Yes, we were aware of that. Just a moment." Connor heard more clacking keys. Good grief, he needed a punching bag or something.

"Er… Detective Reardon? It seems Ms. Shields discharged herself earlier today. Her sister was due to take her home this evening, but instead, Ms. Shields took a taxi. We couldn't hold her for much longer against her will. She has an outpatient appointment in two days. Apparently, her sister will be collecting her from home."

He swore quietly to himself and hung up. Of all the incompetence! He ran to his vehicle, parked underneath police headquarters and unlocked the door meters before he reached it. He was panting, not from physical exertion, but from the thought of Gypsy lying cold in the gutter somewhere. The tires squealed as he reversed the car out of the space as fast as he could.

Would he put the lights on? What the hell, this was urgent. He got the siren going and focused, channeling all of his anger, all of the guilt, the thought of losing her when he'd just met her, into his driving, his concentration a line of sight ahead.

He hoped to hell that she was okay. He wasn't sure if Aaron would be outside her apartment. Hell, he wasn't even sure Aaron had Gypsy's address, but he couldn't take the slightest chance. He needed to see her with his own eyes, touch her, and hold her.

He was so intent on his goal that he was oblivious to the streets and cars around him. He didn't think about getting a parking spot as he usually did. He needed the old faithful weapon and he needed it now.

He fumbled for his key, swearing again as his

fingers became entangled with the items in his pocket. Connor swung the door open and bolted for the bedroom, making for the space under his bed for the second time this week. There it was, staring at him, egging him on. Thank God. He retrieved it from the box, attempting to slow his breathing as he loaded it with the bullets he kept in the same box. With the gun stuffed in his pocket, he walked quickly, almost at a run, back to the front door and headed for the car.

He couldn't wait to see her. He had a feeling something was happening, a bad something.

*****

Wrenching the handle of the canvas bag, he dragged it from the passenger seat and shut the car door. Pools of light on the footpath caught his attention. Skin taut, arms pistons, he made for his final destination. He was slightly out of breath, pulse hammering. This was it, all or nothing.

Standing on the footpath a hundred meters from Gypsy's home, he squinted down the murky deserted street, registering the reflected gold numbers hanging from her mailbox. The dark narrow lane running along the side of the building would be perfect, enveloping him in darkness as it had the night she'd stumbled onto his plan. His pace quickened, a little at first, but then broke into a slow run and felt the impact of his feet hitting concrete vibrating up through his legs. The thought of hurting her tore at him. His chest heaved and his mouth opened sharply as he sucked in breath. He nudged the gate open with one knee, looking around as he did so. Not a soul in sight.

His footsteps were quiet as the incline slowed him. Judging the old sash window, he padded through the rear yard carefully, mentally weighing and measuring the situation.

He pulled the plastic chair to the wall where he jammed it against a downpipe. He stretched his arms up with a grunt. Shit, it was higher than he remembered. He'd work it out. He was determined to get in and leave his message. Once that was done, he'd set himself up in comfort for the flash, the jolt and unexpected blow to come. He couldn't wait to witness the look on the stupid bitch's face.

He looked forward to the squirming, the pain and screams. First, he needed to get through the damn window. Not only was it higher than he'd remembered when he'd cased the place with Stewie, but the chair wasn't tall enough to leverage his body up and through it.

In the dim light from across the lane way, he saw a brick jutting out from the wall, casting a shadow over the others. It could give him the leverage he needed to get up over and in. Standing on the chair that gave slightly under his weight, and with his hands pushed against the wall, Aaron moved his right foot over the brick. The toe of his running shoe stretched and creased as he pushed up. Every muscle strained as he thrust up to grab hold of the sash window. The struggle was worth it. Panting, he heaved the rest of his body up, grunting as he pulled his weight across to perch precariously on the ledge. He felt the weight of the window move upwards grudgingly. It was heavier than he thought. As the frame lifted and reached its peak, the weight of it slammed back down, landing on his sore left knee. He bit down on his bottom lip suppressing a primal scream feeling it resonate in his throat.

The last thing he needed was to attract the attention of meddling neighbors.

Still his leg hurt like fucking hell.

Taking a deep breath, he pushed upward again, feeling the weight of it give and the wooden frame scraped as he raised it high enough to gain entry. The bathroom was dark and hushed like a lifeless cave.

He swung his knees across to dangle his feet into the bathroom. As he searched downward for a solid surface, the soles of his running shoes didn't make contact with a single object.

Damn.

His legs swung in emptiness. He dragged the bag up and over the window ledge.

Not now, idiot, get on with it. There'll be a toilet there somewhere, probably just a foot or two below. Jump!

He called out in shock as he landed feet first into a bath filled with water, cold and dank.

His foot slid to the bottom of the bath, landing him on his back. He jerked up clumsily, the pain rearing up his leg.

"Fuck!"

The surprise of the cold water and the pain of a wrenched ankle registered. He was soaked up his armpits.

Goddamn that bitch to hell.

The water sloshed as he stood up, grasping onto the wall to get his bearings. His breath came out in a rush as he stomped out onto the now slippery tiled floor. He grabbed onto the door handle with his right hand, using the leverage to stagger through the hallway into her lounge room. Thank fuck he was out and had shaken off the watery shock.

Stupid fucking slut.

He'd show her.

Fury building, he headed toward the lounge, and paused to wring out his jumper. To his immediate right were stairs, and at the top of them, on the first left would be her bedroom, according to the plans Stewie had got hold of. At least that dumb fuck had some uses.

At the bottom of the stairs, he bent forward from the waist, his left hand gripping the railing as he got his breath back. There were only twelve steps. If he hadn't hurt his fucking ankle, he could have run up them.

The wet seams of his jeans were rubbing on the cold skin of his thighs. As soon as the dumb bitch got here, he'd make her pay, big time.

His legs felt like lead as he dragged himself up the stairs. He noticed a pile of papers flung across the top, typical. The dirty whore was too lazy to clean up after herself.

He'd planned on leaving some more of the post it notes for her downstairs, but his wet landing had meant a change of plan.

He'd heard via Stewie's grapevine that the neurotic cow left post it notes across her kitchen to remind her to turn appliances off. So he'd decided he'd take them down and leave some notes of his own. She deserved to have the shit scared out of her. He'd planned on waiting for her upstairs, torturing her, at his mercy.

He reached into his pocket, feeling the soggy mass of post it notes disintegrating there. He threw up his right foot, and then he brought it down hard onto what he thought was a wooden stairway.

A fucking trap.

The pictures on the wall bounced and moved, ricocheting off one another.

A furious, blood-curdling scream ripped the walls apart, his scream.

Falling backwards onto his ass, he drew his left foot up to the top platform. He reached for his right ankle encased in a rabbit trap. Metal fangs bit into his skin with the movement. Rearing his head back, he let out another scream of agony.

The teeth had latched on hard; no way could he pull free. If he did, he knew the blood would pour and he'd bleed to death. He gritted his teeth and closed his eyes before letting out a high-pitched wail that he was sure would lift the roof.

He leaned against a wooden post at the top of the stairs and gripped it, hoping to get his body up somehow.

He'd kill her now. Earlier, he'd figured he'd simply scare and hurt her for as long as possible without any idea of murder. The fucking trap had changed his mind, no mucking around with games anymore.

He pushed his way over to the bedroom doorway and levered the door open with his body weight. The bed was directly in front, the green glow from a large screened alarm clock casting an eerie light across the bed. He fell backwards onto it with a grunt, hoisting up his ankle onto the bed complete with trap where he moaned as it made contact with the bed.

His breath came in ragged bursts. He leaned across to turn off the alarm clock. The glow reminded him far too much of the light cast by the television on the night his home burned to the ground, taking his mother with it.

Electrical current surged through his body and he trembled and shook, almost biting off his tongue. As his hand was pushed away from the source, he trembled, feeling real fear for the first in a long time. The bitch deserved more than he gave her. She deserved to die, and die slowly.

Then he lost consciousness.

When he came to, the hard faced bitch was standing over him smiling, electrical wire in hand.

She'd been through his bag.

He was fucked.

*****

Finally.

I was home.

I heard the taxi pull away as I slammed the front door shut with the sole of my shoe.

I dropped my bag beside me, hearing a thud as it landed, and tilted my head to listen for the screams of pain. I wasn't looking forward to inflicting pain, especially pain that involved my loved ones, but after the hell Aaron had put us through, it had to be done. He had to be stopped.

I felt my pulse pumping in my neck, a freight train out of control.

Fear gripped me, tightening my stomach and I sucked in a sharp breath.

Had something gone wrong? Maybe Aaron had intercepted them. A picture of Renee and Paul tied up and gagged flashed before me.

Calm down, Gypsy.

I focused on slowing down my breathing, reining

in my pulse.

I leaned down to unzip my bag, fishing for the scalpel and tens-electrical impulse machine I'd swiped from the hospital. That hadn't been easy, but then again, who would suspect a brain injury patient on the brink of discharge would flog hospital equipment for her own nefarious ends?

Obviously, not the hospital staff.

Carrying my stash, I walked over to the hallway closet, swinging the door open hopefully.

The hunting rifle was still there.

I hooked it under my armpit and headed for the stairs. My pulse was no longer hammering. In fact, I felt quite calm. As I reached the stairs, I saw that part of the plan had worked. There was water everywhere, a trail leading upwards. I followed it to the top and found the last step had been removed.

The trap must have gotten him and the plan we'd carefully worked out had worked. I headed for the bedroom.

I walked in cautiously and there he was, flaked out on the bed.

His foot was caught in the trap, which was hanging at the end of the bed. His head hung to one side, and as he breathed, he sucked the bed linen into his open mouth. I dragged in the blue workbag he'd dropped on the landing at the top of the stairs, and leaned down to see electrical wire springing from it. Dropping the tens machine, scalpel and hunting rifle, I grasped the handle ready to loop it around his wrists and pull the wire tight.

Aaron's eyes flickered open, his face changing color as he realized who I was.

"Didn't turn out the way you expected, then?" My

right hand was on my waist above my cockily jutting hip. I leaned over quickly and had the wire around his hands now, and pulled it tighter, listening as he called out.

"You fucking bitch!" Spittle launched from his mouth, and his face contorted, purple mottle beginning to spread across its whiteness.

"Now then, Aaron, that's not the way to make friends, is it? Temper temper." His hands were secure, but as I stepped back, he tried to sit up. Aaron managed to lift his shoulder from the bed before sagging back. With his right ankle trapped, he was going nowhere, just as I'd hoped.

My hands were shaking, feet wide apart as I pushed his hands away from me. The fury raged through my veins, gaining momentum like a train speeding out of control.

He tried getting up again, his stomach flexing as he yet again tried lifting his head from the bed, then landed back with a howl.

"Frustrated?" I said, warming to my task. "I understand completely. That's how I felt when I woke up in the hospital. Confused? Trapped? Suck it up, princess, you won't hurt anyone else again. I'll make damned sure of it."

I pulled down his track suit pants, which stunk. Shit. Someone should have told him to bathe.

Keeping my gaze fixed on the skunk, I leaned down and curled my fingers around the tens machines handle. Glancing down, I pressed the switch and saw the screen light up.

"This one's from me to you. I'm sure Joanne Seyers would be interested in watching, but she's laid up in the hospital recovering from a blow to the head.

Sound familiar, fuck face?"

I attached three of the pads to his scrotum, one on either side and one underneath. I was repelled, but duty called. The pads were connected to the grey plastic console with thin wires. His scrotum matched his face—hideously ugly. Sure, he might be fucked up and troubled, but no one forced him to kidnap one woman, and leave me for dead after ramming me with his van. He needed to understand that no evil deed went unpunished, and my fury had taken hold of me sufficiently that I knew with certainty, I would be the one to administer it.

His eyes widened.

"You stupid fucking bitch, I should have killed you!" His howl was loud enough to shake the door.

"You're right, you should have killed me." My legs were planted wide and I bared my teeth. "That's the problem with telepaths. You can never predict what we'll do next. We have a habit of wandering into dark laneways for no apparent reason." I heard the dryness in my voice, its timbre deep and threatening. "Plus, we can sometimes get a read on what you're up to." I leaned down to lift the second tens machine with slightly smaller pads onto the bed.

He gave a high pitched shriek, opening his mouth so wide I could see the back of his throat.

"Listen here, slime ball, irritate me again with your pathetic wailing and I'll gag you, and I'd really rather not. I've got a lot to do and only a bit of time to do it. So can it."

He started to cry and shake, his shoulders shaking, but at least his screams had simmered down to a whimper.

I revised my plan to place some of the pads on the

webbing between his fingers, choosing his eyelids instead.

I separated the magnetic pads on the second machine, and leaned over his body, inhaling another waft of his body odor. He tried pushing me off, rolling his shoulders from side to side, which bashed against my forearms, so I leaned a knee on his chest, increasing his mangled cries.

At last, the pads were on. It was payback time.

After lining the small consoles side by side on the bed, I squatted and turned up the power intensity button. Small pulses were therapeutic and sending a tiny amount of electrical current through the muscles could offer pain relief. Full intensity was used in only extreme cases to alleviate intense pain, and this was definitely an extreme case.

I swung the knob hard to the right. I was rewarded with his agony, the deep voiced animal cry bouncing around the corners and ceiling.

"That was for my niece, remember her? You followed her home, you piece of shit. Haven't you heard, numb nuts? Hell hath no fury like a telepath scorned. You should have left us alone."

16

As Connor sped away from his home, he felt something gnawing at him inside his chest. It was like a curtain parting, unlike anything he had sensed before.

Yet another one of the pieces of information he had withheld from Gypsy was that he suspected he had abilities of his own.

He remained unaware of his manic breathing and muttering under his breath. His neck corded as he beat at the steering wheel with the heel of his palm.

The ability to block thoughts and prevent others from gaining any insight into what was going on inside, had been a big factor in the marriage break up. He was so used to shutting people out that he'd shut Jill out, too. It hadn't been a conscious choice, purely instinct, but it had wounded her so badly they'd never recovered. It was something he'd pushed to the periphery, a kernel of knowledge he rarely thought about. Until he'd met Gypsy.

This attempt to form a crack and peek inside his world was pretty intense though, determined, dogged, insistent.

He scratched a cheek and rubbed a fist over the front of his shirt. He realized she'd somehow forced her way in. He could see her pictures, her messages.

It was Gypsy.

The connection he'd sensed on the night they met was probably a part of that. When she'd told him about her abilities, he'd barely batted an eyelid. He'd had similar experiences many years ago, but blocked them out. Like the night as a young boy that his mother had held a party at home. He'd retreated to his bedroom for over an hour before hunger had forced him out. The ordinary looking middle-aged woman sitting at a table in the corner of the dining room caught his eye.

"Got a minute?" said the middle-aged medium. He wasn't sure and so didn't answer, eyeing off his sandwich with hunger.

"Take a seat. It won't hurt, I promise."

He had his doubts but shuffled over to the chair before her. He sat unmoving as she spoke to him, flicking cards across the table, which meant little to a thirteen-year-old boy.

"You have the gift but you don't want it. You can't deny it forever, you know." She peered at him across her glasses. Not sure what to say to that, he said nothing.

"Your skills as a sentinel might come in handy, but at some point, you're going to have to let someone in."

He found his voice, which was squeaky and annoying. "What's a sentinel?"

"A protector, a guard, it's like a force field you put out. You can prevent psychics from getting a read on you, or anyone else for that matter."

He'd gotten up from the seat and simply walked away. She didn't know what she was talking about, and he pushed the knowledge away to the deepest recesses of his mind. It wasn't something he wanted to talk about, but it certainly made sense, striking a chord within him, a truth that rang like a bell.

So now, when he felt the tugging, the pinging he knew it was Gypsy.

She was in trouble.

Holy hell.

He viewed the picture she had used to break through, forcing it before him.

She was at home, had discharged herself early, of that much he was certain. Aaron had climbed in through a window, thinking he could lie in wait for her, but she'd set a trap and was torturing him slowly.

Good God.

He pulled over quickly to send a text message to Ian Robson. Maybe he could get there before him. He jerked his foot down on the accelerator.

Ian replied within seconds. He was on the other side of the city. *Damn.* He'd be there as fast as he could, but even with a siren, it would take him thirty minutes minimum. Connor knew that if he hammered it, he'd be there within five to ten minutes at the most.

If he didn't get there soon, either Aaron or Gypsy would wind up dead.

*****

"Calm down? Calm down, *I am—*"

"Stop, Mum!"

Renee had never seen Leah like this. Breathing fast, punctuating her words with an occasional bang of her hands on the steering wheel, she was going off like a rocket with no direction, leaving a burning trail of octane in her wake.

"Mum, that's it. This is only making things worse. Plus you're driving, and it's not good to drive like this."

"Worse! How can it get any bloody worse, answer me that? Your dad's buggered off with a young floozy and now thinks he can just turn up whenever he feels like it and all is forgiven, while I work all the hours God sends to keep food on the table. Now my sister has disappeared, probably lying on her floor unconscious while some nutcase drags her–"

"*No*! That's it, Mum, no more, *stop*!"

The shock of Renee's outburst silenced Leah. Renee watched as Leah took a deep breath and tried to will the calmness into her body, her lips forming a tight O as she blew the tension away.

"That's it, deep breaths. Good work, Mum."

They drove along for another minute or two, silence restored. After a while, the silence reassured Renee, the slight rocking motion triggering a semi-conscious trance. With a jolt, she came to and saw they weren't driving to her aunt's place. They were going home.

"Where are we going?"

"What?" Leah was still distracted.

"Where are we *going*?"

"For God's sake, Renee, we're going home, isn't that bleeding obvious?"

She couldn't believe it.

"But you were just carrying on like a pork chop about Gypsy at her place on her own, and now you're driving home?"

There was a long silence while Leah fought the battle with her own overflowing emotions, and ultimately won.

"You know what she's like about that cat. She treats it like a damn human. If I go back to her place, she'll ask me why I didn't bring the cat with me and I don't want another bloody scene like we had at the hospital."

"But you said she needs our help."

Renee had a feeling Leah wouldn't say why she was delaying the trip to Gypsy's. She must have some idea, and was too scared to face it. Renee, however, figured the trap they'd laid would do the trick and Gypsy would be fine. She couldn't tell Leah any of it, and wished she'd stop being so hysterical.

But collecting the cat before checking on Gypsy? Leah was in denial and had worked herself up to an almost hysterical state by delaying the confirmation she didn't want to hear.

"*She does*! She just won't accept it. She's as stubborn as a damn mule, and she's driving me up the wall, I swear, and maybe you're right, I might be overreacting a tad. It's just that sometimes the pressure gets all too bloody much. I know you understand, honey, everything's over the top today. We'll pick up the damn cat and be in and out in a flash."

Good grief, she really had lost it. No point in going on about it, though. Renee knew if she did, it would be all downhill from there.

"Okay, Mum, we'll pick the cat up from our place and take him to Gypsy's," said Renee, doing her best to suppress a sigh.

The car pulled into the driveway. Leah's hand seemed to shake as she fumbled to get the key in the lock, or was Renee imagining it?

Leah dropped her bags on the floor while she opened the door. She stepped inside and went looking for the cat, bending over, clucking her tongue, only stopping to call out, "Here pussycat, here puss." Renee tried not to roll her eyes.

"Should I grab the cat food then and put it in a bag, Mum?"

"We have to find the damn cat first, but yes, do that and then see if you can find the kitty litter. Oh shit, where's the damn box to put the cat in?"

Renee grabbed a plastic bag and shoved the cat food in, then spied the kitty litter in the laundry. She wrinkled her nose as she picked it up with one hand. *Ew, disgusting.* She held it out in front of her as far as she could and walked outside to the rubbish bin. What a job. She emptied it out, trying not to pull her ugly face, but it was practically impossible. It stunk to high heaven. Returning inside, she slammed the front door closed.

Mum had found Jerry. He was eating from his bowl on the kitchen floor, which had just been filled up, and she was sitting a few meters away on the edge of a kitchen chair chewing her nails.

"Mum, do you need a hand with the cat?"

"Of *course,* I do. I'm just waiting for it to finish eating so it doesn't claw me again when I try to put it in that damn box. Jerry scratched me, the little bugger, when I picked him up from Gypsy's place."

Not sure what to do, Renee eventually headed to the pantry and grabbed a snack. A muesli bar would do for now. She opened it and started chewing.

As expected, Leah had grown impatient and grabbed the cat before it finished eating. Of course, it scratched her, and she screamed at the top of her lungs and shoved it in the box.

"Mum! Gentle…"

"Oh, not now, Renee!"

Leah was sitting on the chair crying, her right hand up, trying to hide her contorted face and failing miserably.

Renee stood inches away from Leah. She put one hand on her mum's shoulder and Leah's head went further down, until it connected gently with her chest.

"Oh, I'm sorry."

"It's all right. Seriously, please don't say you're sorry."

"I wish I was a better mum…"

Oh no, not this again. Renee knew this was a culmination of all the garbage lately. Renee felt a rush of warmth, wanting to comfort her mother.

"Don't say that, Mum, seriously…"

Leah was at the sniffling stage, so with a pat, Renee went to get her a tissue from the box on the bench.

"It'll be all right. That's what you always tell me, remember?"

"I know, I know." She was calming a bit now, the flow of tears slowing. "It's just, I'm meant to be the strong one. It's my job to look after you, and here I am…"

"Mum, don't be silly. I told you we need to stick together. Let's go see Gypsy so she can give us both an earful."

Leah managed a thin smile as she looked up at her daughter. "When the hell did you get so smart? Or maybe I wasn't paying attention properly…"

Renee rubbed her mum's back until Leah picked up her keys, threw them into her handbag, and leaned down to pick up the handle of the cat box.

"Come on, let's take this bag of bones over to meet her royal highness," Leah said. Renee knew everything would be okay, especially if the plan they'd set up kicked in.

*****

Although I'd put the scalpel in the bag, I couldn't bring myself to use it on Aaron. Not only did it cross the line between retribution and psychotic, but I wouldn't do well witnessing that much blood. Glancing across at the workbag, I saw the slight sheen of the crowbar slung across the top, dark heavy metal calling my name.

Now that could be interesting.

I gripped one end so tightly my fingers turned white. Metal jarred against clanging metal as I pulled up the crowbar.

The bastard hadn't even bothered to wash the blood off.

"Look what I found, Aaron. Ringing any bells?"

His eyes were round, his face ashen. Yep, he recognized it all right.

"I'm feeling indecisive right now. My problem is…what do I do with this crowbar? Do I swing it back as high as I can, smashing down until it caves your skull in? Or do I continue for round two of the tens machine? Both sound appealing, especially because either way, you'll get what you deserve and can't hurt anyone else. What do you think?"

"Take off the pads, bitch face, fucking take 'em *off*!" His animal screams were at a frenzied pitch.

The curses sealed it for me. I picked up the crowbar and swung it, feeling its weight and wondered if I could really do it. As evil as he was, killing was different altogether. I wanted him to suffer, but I wasn't fully convinced of murder no matter how much I thought he deserved it.

All I wanted at that moment was to hurt him as he hurt me.

I stood beside his exhausted form, swinging the rod back and forth, legs slightly apart in a golfer stance.

"The others were for Joanne, and Renee, but this one's just from me to you."

As I pushed my hips out to gain momentum, I heard an almighty bang downstairs. Someone had forced the door in, and I knew who it was.

Connor.

#

Connor ran away from the car letting the door fall closed and he bounded up the steps to Gypsy's front door, flicking sweat from his hands. He didn't think she'd answer, but he pounded on the front door regardless. The screams of his nephew filtered down through the door.

Aaron was in agony that much was certain.

He pounded harder.

"Gypsy! Open up!"

If she was as determined as he believed, he had to get in there damn quickly.

He took a couple of steps back and rammed the old wooden door with his shoulder, and it bounced slightly in its frame but didn't give.

Heading halfway back across the front garden, he stared at his target before he ran toward it and shouldered the door again, feeling his body weight make contact, and was shocked to feel the door open with a loud snap.

He remembered with chagrin his comment to Gypsy the night they met.

"It's not like you see on television. It's not all kicking in doors."

He spied a staircase at the end of the short hallway. Connor ran through the hallway in two strides, bounding up the stairs to her bedroom.

There she was, mouth set in a line of fury, eyes dark and bloodshot, hair wild.

His blood went cold. She was obviously set in her mission of destroying his nephew.

He took a tentative step toward her.

"Gypsy, no, not like this." He caught his breath, conscious of keeping his voice quiet, calming and in stark contrast to the blood racing through his limbs, palms facing her, hoping to soothe and steady her.

The hair billowed around her face as she turned to him. He could almost see the electricity, making her hair crackle.

"If not like this, then how? He'll get eight years max, and be out in two. How the hell is that justice for anyone?"

She'd at least hung her head and lowered the crowbar a little. It was now at her waist rather than eye level. He could hear her breathing loudly through her throat and nose, and her chest heaved as she struggled to control it.

Connor moved closer to her, hands away from his body.

"Is this what you want? Jail time? You'll be arrested, Gypsy, and I know you don't want that. Think about Renee, your sister, about me…"

She turned to him, every inch of her screaming at him to keep his distance. Gypsy was pumped, a live wire ready to strike.

"Hang tight, Aaron, I'll get to you." Connor said. Touching her elbow lightly, he moved her to the chair at the bottom of the bed. "Sit down for just a minute. Please. I promise you'll get justice. I'll make sure of it."

*****

Luckily, for Aaron, Connor had arrived and talked me down. I was ready to send Aaron into oblivion and was struggling with the impact of what had happened and what I now realized I was capable of. I dropped the crowbar and stared at my trembling hands. The adrenaline of sweet revenge had sustained me, but as I took deep breaths and began to calm down, I realized that Connor was right. The slime ball wasn't worth being locked up away from my loved ones.

I watched as Connor sat beside his nephew and spoke to him in a quiet rumbling voice, probably attempting to soothe him. He didn't sound like he was having the impact he'd hoped for in light of Aaron's whimpers of pain and contorted face.

I wondered how Connor was coping with all of this. It was one thing to be a cop, another to have a close family member turn out to be a kidnapper and stalker rolled into one filthy package.

I'd known it was Aaron, instinctively and subconsciously detected it when Connor visited me in hospital, but I buried it deep. I should have known more, trusted my instincts and followed them more closely. Despite the terror, the blood racing through my veins, every nerve ending on high alert, some small part of me was relieved that Connor hadn't been the bad guy I feared. In fact, I didn't want to admit that I'd ever questioned his motives. How was he coping? How did a person go on functioning after finding out that someone they loved, trusted, and cared for across an entire lifetime, had gone wrong like this?

"If I untie you, can I trust you? You won't do anything stupid?" Aaron's eyes were bulging, his voice hoarse.

"Course I fucking won't. Keep the psycho bitch away from me." His voice indicated his cries had reduced from terror to anger.

I turned to Connor, incredulous. "You're not serious? You're going to *untie* him?"

When Connor spoke again, his voice cracked. "I'm thinking about it. He's looking at jail time, no matter how this plays out." He stared at the hunting rifle beside the bed. I hadn't got to using that. Truth be told, I had no idea how. It was Mark's and had been sitting in the cupboard for God knew how long.

"If I untie your hands, don't let me down, Aaron. You'll need an ambulance for that ankle. I'll call it in. Ian will be here soon." Connor's voice was dry and croaky, but in that instant, it sounded safe, reassuring, a beacon of hope. The relief surged. This might turn out okay, just maybe.

Aaron's head snapped up. Despite the grimace of pain written across his face, his bloodshot stare was fixed on his uncle.

"Ian? Ian who?" However, Connor already had the phone to his ear.

"I have a suspect injured on the scene. We'll need an ambulance." Connor paused as he looked across at Aaron. "Right ankle caught in a rabbit trap." Another pause. "That's right, a rabbit trap."

After what was probably a minute or so, but felt like seconds, I heard the thud of boots on the carpeted hall downstairs, followed by the thump of what was likely a heavyset person heading up stairs.

A dark haired overweight man wearing glasses stood in the doorway. A gun hung in his right hand.

"Connor, you found him." He sounded out of breath.

"Yeah." Connor turned to face the man who was obviously his partner.

Aaron rubbed his groin. "You piece of *shit*. It was you, ya fucking scumbag, wasn't it? What color is his fucking car?" He jerked his chin at his uncle and tried again to get up with no success.

"What? Why?" Connors hand rested on his belt.

"Because this fat fucker's name was on the report. You were the guy Tiran mentioned before she hung up. Dark haired, blue car, no uniform." He reached across and dug around in the bag, his hand emerging with a crumpled wet set of papers. "Look familiar?"

Ian leaned, in what I thought was an attempt to snatch the report from Aaron's hand. Instead, he grabbed Aaron's collar and hurled Aaron up, dragging him across the bed. Ian spat through gritted teeth.

"You kidnapped a police employee, you fucking scumbag."

Aaron screamed in pain, his hands clawing at Ian without making contact.

Connor bounded over, attempting to separate them.

"That's enough! The ambulance will be here soon. Let's get Aaron's injuries treated, and then we'll work this mess out."

Ian Robson let go of Aaron and gazed at Connor,

his mouth open slightly. He rubbed the back of his neck and bit his lip.

"What color's your car then, fuckwit?" Aaron's face was red, eyes bulging.

Connor mumbled hoarsely, "It's blue."

"I spoke to Tiran one last time to warn her about the list. When we were talking, she said someone pulled up and I asked if it was a cop. She said no, some bloke she didn't recognize. A bloke with dark hair had pulled up in a blue car. It was *him*!"

Connor's face was ashen. "Ian? What the hell is he talking about?"

"You don't understand. They were chasing me. I played a few rounds of poker and if I didn't pay 'em back… It was just here and there, nothing major."

Connor inched forward. "So what, you swiped cash and weapons from crime scenes?"

Aaron did his best to shuffle across to the edge of the bed.

"Yeah, he didn't want the report to hit the open air, especially if his name was listed as a bent cop. When he couldn't find it at the factory, he went to visit my missus and killed her. Didn't you, you piece of shit?" said Aaron through gritted teeth.

"Listen, low life…"

Aaron grabbed at the hunting rifle on the floor. I saw it in slow motion, the gun pointed at Ian Robson, the look of satisfaction on Aaron's face as his arm locked alongside the weapon and he pulled the trigger.

The room exploded. A sound shook the walls, the

floors vibrating. My body was shoved backward in the chair.

I saw Connor pull his gun out. Aaron's body jerked backward, his arms falling forward. His eyes registered a look of betrayal. His hand went to his stomach where the first purplish bud had appeared.

Ian was hit between the eyes and he had fallen backwards, his head hitting the cupboard before he landed on the ground with a sickening smash.

Then it was quiet. My ears were ringing, and the smell of sulfur and ammonia stung my nose. Connor was still.

It had been so fast that it took a second to register it was over. Connor stepped sideways. After a moment, he sat beside me on the floor.

It took a moment before I could speak. Aaron was still screaming.

"I, I, I can't believe that just happened. I thought you were going to shoot him in the leg or the shoulder or something…"

"He was never going to stop. Ever." Connor was fidgeting, his knee jiggling. "As for Ian, my God…" I rubbed at my wrists and looked up at him. His face was pale underneath and I saw the grey marks of insomnia forming under his eyes. It was difficult for him to meet my gaze at the moment, but then, he'd just done something that neither of us would ever forget.

"This has been harder on you than I ever thought, but then I had the wrong idea…" I didn't want to tell him that I'd ever doubted his motives and at one point had suspected he was behind the abductions. I turned to him, and draped an arm around his shoulders, finally allowing myself to turn and embrace him feeling the warmth. He felt good and I let out a long breath.

I closed my eyes, feeling his pulse spinning out of control beneath my cheek. The lights outside cut through the darkness and I saw the red and blue lights spinning and shining through the bedroom window.

The ambulance had arrived.

17

I heard Leah long before I saw her. The paramedic had draped a blanket around my shoulders as I sipped on hot sweet tea. Her screams were barbaric. Her naked anguish was all encompassing. Held back by the police tape and surrounded by nosy neighbors and news vans lining the street, she must have feared the worst.

I made my way to the door to speak to the officer posted on my front porch.

I leaned across to get his attention, my hair in disarray and one shoe falling off. I struggled to get it back on when she spotted me. She called "*Ah*! My sister, oh, my God, Gypsy, you're *alive*."

She threw her arms around me in a vicelike grip and as she held on, her squeeze was so tight I struggled to breathe. I shook my head and closed my eyes. As I held my sister, I realized my hands were trembling.

Her torso convulsed as she began to sob. She cried the tears that wouldn't come to me. We'd truly achieved what I had yearned for. We were sisters again. I knew she loved me. The thought of losing each other had brought home to us how it would feel.

I pulled away and grasping her shoulders studied her.

"Wipe your face. You look like panda girl. Your makeup has run."

That at least brought a small smile to her tear streaked face. She wiped the tears away with her fingers.

"Goddamn you, Gypsy, you scared the shit out of me. What the hell were you thinking discharging yourself?" I looked down at Renee by Leah's side and she smiled faintly as I grabbed her hand.

"I had a rough plan. I'm glad it worked out and I'm in one piece, kind of."

Leah smoothed down her hair.

"Next time, let me know before you go off half-cocked, okay? You damn loose cannon." Her shoulders slumped and she turned her body away slightly.

"Okay, Leah, I'll make a note for my files." I grabbed her hand that had fallen by her side.

I held her gaze as I squeezed her hand. "I'm going to have to go inside and finish making a statement. It's like Central Station in there."

"All right, meet me at my place when you're done, okay? We've got some catching up to do." Leah placed her arm on Renee's shoulder, ushering her back to their car.

I headed inside.

As I wandered in, I passed two technicians carrying a body bag, which I assumed contained all that was left of Ian Robson.

Connor was talking with two men whose clothes looked like a throwback to the seventies, one of them with hair plastered to his head. The unknown man's hands were waving around madly, his voice urgent and insistent.

Probably explaining the whole corruption and lost report saga. It was moments like these that I was grateful I didn't work in the police force, far too much pressure and intensity. Then again, I had almost been killed twice. I didn't want to go through this ever again. Thankfully, Connor would explain to the powers that be, why I had Aaron tied up, and I'd mentioned it in my statement too.

I sat down on my comfortable couch, scrunching my butt into the groove.

Connor nodded his head, their conversation drawing to a close.

Connor turned. "Okay, later then, Bittern," he said. I felt the couch give a little as he sat down.

I looked at him, relieved to see some color had returned to his face.

"What's the plan? Is there one?"

I saw a grimace twist across his face. "I don't know how I'll explain this to Jill. I think Christie has an idea though. Ian and I interviewed her a couple of days ago."

I looked down. "Yeah, Ian."

"I'm still numb. We always said that people could surprise us, but I didn't think that meant he would shock me like this." He winced and rubbed a fist across his chest. "The irony is that his name was never on the confidential list of potentially corrupt cops."

"It wasn't?"

"No, there was an Ian Braithwaite, but Ian didn't know that I guess. Aaron got it wrong. Ian was paranoid, and when he assumed the worst, well…" Connor's expression was slack his eyes dull and he stared down at his empty hands.

"So what happens from here?" I placed my hand on his back.

"Aaron's in the hospital. From there, he'll go to court and face charges. Police killers don't do well in jail. He'll live. It takes time to bleed out from a stomach wound and the ambulance got here in time."

"I'm still numb. I can't believe you shot him..."

"Yeah, well, blood isn't always thicker than water, especially after what he did, the pain he put so many people through. At first, I blamed myself, thought I wasn't supportive enough, it was my fault." His shoulders were drooped and his voice broke slightly. "I did everything I could before I realized he made a series of choices. This was his choice and his alone. He was never going to change. He'll be locked up for a long time"

I asked a question he probably didn't want to answer.

"Ian's corruption?"

Connor nodded. "He'd kept his secret for a long time. He must have practiced the art of hiding crime scene theft and gambling debts so long, he became an expert. He didn't want anyone to find out about the internal affairs investigation or the list."

Connor's stare was distant. "I never picked him as a killer. That's what burns, but maybe he didn't think he was capable of it. I'm guessing his decision to kill Tiran was spontaneous rather than planned."
Connor's voice sounded flat and lifeless, expression slack, eyes dull. "His name wasn't even on the damn list, I checked." Head down, Connor shook his head,

lips pressed together.

I moved closer. "Do you know how many times I wished we could have started things off differently? With a light hearted coffee somewhere, you know, like normal people do?"

One corner of his mouth moved upwards and he jerked his head up. "Yeah, me too."

"I guess something positive came out of this though." I reached for his hand, which felt warm and alive.

"Oh, yeah, what's that?" Connor's brown eyes were beginning to show traces of life again. He placed his hand on mine.

"Meeting me, of course." I felt the delicious rush of his fingers as they brushed my cheek.

"That's true," he said quietly. "Don't they say better late than never? Maybe we can make up for lost time."

As his lips brushed against mine, warm, smooth, and delicious, I knew that we would.

- THE END -